ROADRUNNER MOTEL

E. LYNN

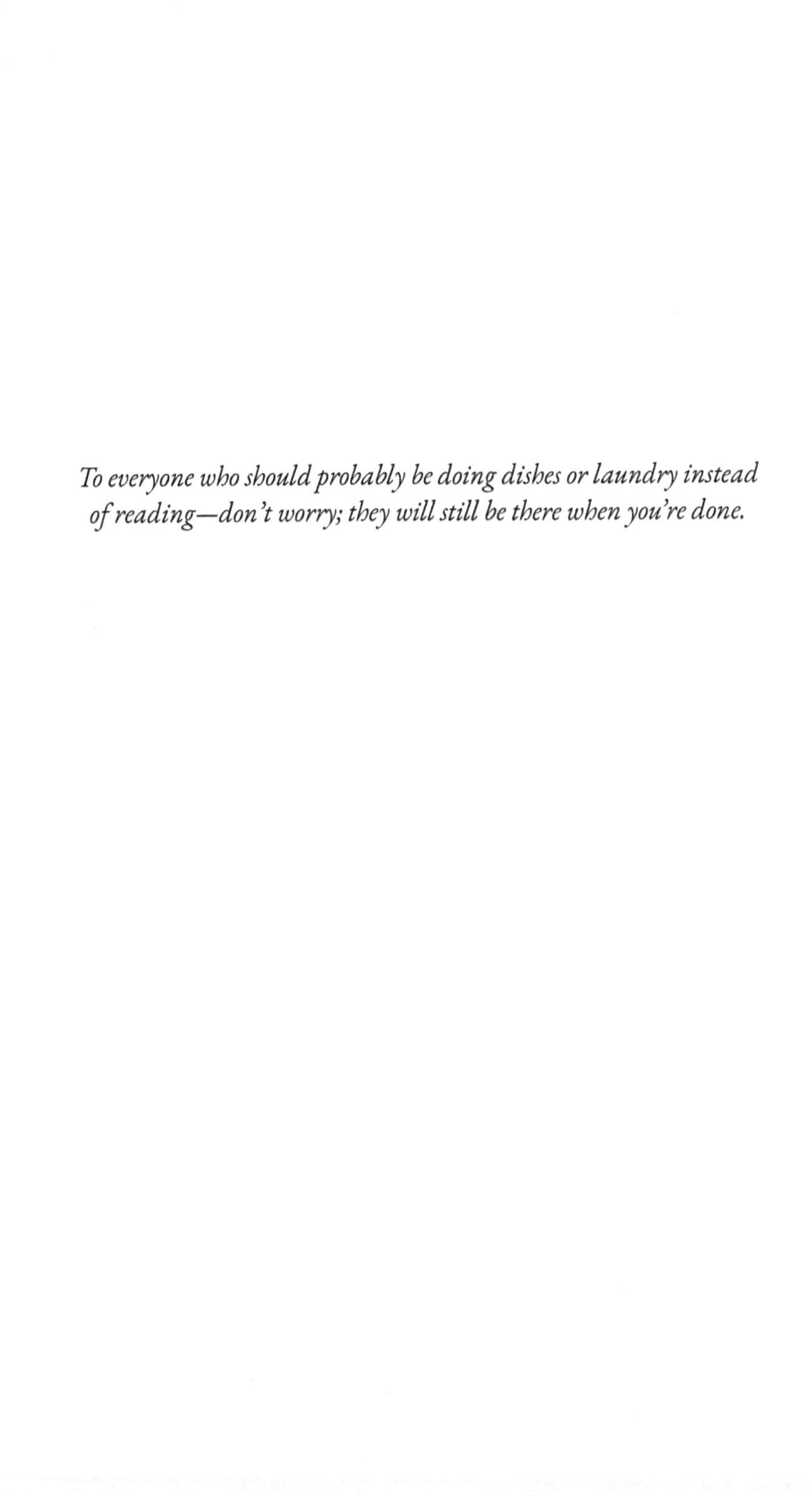

To everyone who should probably be doing dishes or laundry instead of reading—don't worry; they will still be there when you're done.

Reader Reviews

"No spoilers. Read via physical ARC from author.

First I need to give a special thank you to E. Lynn for sending me this ARC. Second I just need to say WOW! This book has triggers and is truly a female's worst nightmare, but oh my gosh this story! I would love to think that I would be as strong as she was in this story, but honestly she amazed me in what she does. The twists and turns in this story has you on the edge of your seat the whole time. I started it late one night, and then instantly had to finish it when I woke up. I could not go any longer to figure out how this ends. I absolutely loved this book, that I would reread this again! Such a quick great read! I cannot wait to read more from E. Lynn!

Would I recommend? YES! If you are okay with the triggers and want a quick thrill read, I highly recommend reading this!"
Goodreads review from Samanthasue218 July 2024

CHAPTER ONE
MARIA, JUNE 29TH

Maria carried her resume with shaking hands as she approached the frosted-glass doors of the conference room—the room that held the opportunity she'd been waiting for, the one she needed to advance in her career. Positions like this rarely opened up, and most of the people in her office had been with the company for longer than she'd been alive.

Releasing a long, steady breath, she raised a trembling hand to push open the door, but she froze at the last minute. Her boss, Dean, was speaking, and she didn't want to interrupt. The last thing she wanted to do was shoot herself in the foot before she even had the chance to get an interview.

"Yes, I know Maria plans on applying," he said in a bored tone. He began to laugh.

He must be on the phone. Hearing her name had her second-guessing her next steps into the conference room. Perhaps it would be best to come back later.

"You know I won't let a skirt take this position." Another barked laugh met her ears.

Breath catching in her throat, she felt her dreams crumbling at her feet. The future she'd been picturing shattered. The shards cut into her heart, leaving her aspirations to bleed out on the tile floor beneath the navy wedges she'd carefully selected that morning while creating a professional image she hoped would convey her capabilities. The care she'd taken in her outfit suddenly seemed silly. She was never going to be able to move up in this company, and that realization had her taking a clumsy step back, tears welling in her eyes.

She bumped into the wall behind her as her cell phone vibrated in her pocket. Without checking the display, she picked up with a distracted, whispered, "Hello?" She choked on the word as it escaped her lips.

"Hey, Maria, I really hate to do this to you," Kameron said, her voice filled with remorse. Before she said anything more, Maria knew where the conversation was headed. "It's about our trip. I'm not going to be able to go with you."

Maria's day was not going to get any better. In fact, she knew the rest of her week was going to be crap.

"I need this break, Kameron," Maria whispered, pleading.

"Maria, I'm sorry. You know I was looking forward to us getting together and just spending time together. But something came up at work. I'm at work now, but I wanted to call and let you know as soon as possible. I'll call you tonight to talk about the hotels we have booked. Love you." Kameron was speaking so fast, Maria wasn't entirely sure what to think first.

"Love you," Maria said as an ache filled her chest. All the things she'd been looking forward to were going up in smoke. It was as if someone had just kicked over the line of dominos that made up Maria's plans and dreams before she'd even had the chance to get them all fully set up.

Still clutching her resume, she walked back to her desk. She needed to let Dean's words process before she did anything crass. She might be pissed—dejected too—but she needed this job. Quitting without a backup plan would be imprudent. She was not foolish enough to allow someone's misogynistic comments to break her.

As she slammed her stapler back down onto her desk, Jared entered her cubicle. It would have been nice to have her own space to hide in, but instead, they had tiny cubicles that allowed each person to not only hear but see one another if they stood up. Privacy was too much to ask for, apparently.

"Apply for the job?" he asked leaning on the edge of her desk. Something about his slimy smile had her hackles rising. Does he already know Dean's thoughts on giving me the promotion?

"Not yet." She moved papers around her desk, trying to appear as normal as possible. The last thing she wanted was for the rumor mill to start. She might work in a predominately male office, but these men knew how to create a web of lies that extended into the corners of each and every cubicle, office, and bathroom.

He tsked at her as if she were a child. "You have to start showing that you want things around here, Maria. No one is going to chase you." He picked at his fingernails. "Not that I think you have a snowball's chance in hell of getting that promotion. It'll be mine." After tapping the edge of her desk, he walked away.

She wished she could think of something snarky to shout at his back. Groaning, she leaned forward and rested her elbows on her desk, head in her hands. Pathetic. Am I really going to let Jared, the man who can't figure out how to match a tie to a suit jacket, tell me what I can and can't do?

"Apparently," she muttered to herself.

Her desk shook, and she was ready to bare her teeth at Jared if he was already back. Snapping her head up, she found herself looking into the ice-blue eyes of her favorite coworker—her surrogate grandfather.

He leaned in conspiratorially. "Don't let that ass dissuade you."

"Pete, how am I going to get anywhere with the good-ol'-boys club still in full swing?"

He nodded as if really contemplating her words. "I have watched you since you started here. You don't back down from anything, and you are able to work out an issue faster than most. I have faith in you."

She scoffed, flopping back in her chair.

"If they're too stupid to hire you for the new position, leave."

"You say it like it's so easy," she whispered, trying to make sure no one else heard her.

"For you, I bet it would be. No one wants to hire an old coot like me who's only ever worked one place." Rising from the edge of her desk, he placed a hand on her shoulder. "Take your vacation to think it over. Is this the place you want to be?"

She knew his question was rhetorical, but she still wanted to answer it. Yes. This is the place I want to be.

Right?

CHAPTER TWO
HANNAH, JUNE 30TH

After relaxing on the beach of the resort for the fourth day in a row, Hannah was bored. She loved to sunbathe, but she didn't feel it was necessary to spend every waking moment baking to a crisp. She couldn't be exposed to the sun too long before her cheeks turned rosy and her skin began to dry and itch. The curses of being blond and fair-skinned.

Their group had been warned to always remain on the resort. She'd wanted to vacation in Florida, but none of the others had—they'd figured there would be far too many people. Her parents had given her an ultimatum—if she wanted them to fund the trip, she needed to go with a group. "Safety in numbers," they'd said. Since she was still in college and her part-time job barely afforded her the simplest of luxuries—and she'd been far too excited the last time she could afford to splurge on a cheesecake—she didn't have much of a choice.

Your young adult years are meant to be enjoyed, right? She was beginning to regret her decision. She could have just driven to North Carolina, done some hiking, and gone to the coast. Then she wouldn't have been trapped in an impossibly boring situation. Jenny and Kenzie wanted to do nothing but lie on the beach, while

Cassidy didn't care what they did as long as she could bring a book along.

Sighing, Hannah pushed herself back as far as she could in the covered chair she'd claimed that morning. It was unbearably hot, and the others didn't appear to be planning to move any time soon. Staring out at the ocean ahead, she couldn't deny the relaxation the sound of the waves brought her. But a restlessness remained. Adventure—that was what she wanted.

"Han," Kenzie said, "can you try to have fun?"

"I thought we would do something more than lay on the beach all day every day." She hated the irritation seared into her tone.

"We will." The smirk on Kenzie's face sent anxiety and fear into Hannah's soul. Kenzie's ideas of fun usually meant Hannah was doing something she didn't want to.

"Tonight is going to be great," Jenny added in her high timbre. Jenny was essentially a cheerleader for Kenzie—she encouraged and cheered on every one of Kenzie's plans.

Confused, Hannah looked from one friend's face to the next. Jenny and Kenzie exchanged conspiratorial glances while Cassidy barely removed her eyes from her new romance novel.

"How so?" Hannah asked suspiciously.

"We're going to the tiki bar when it opens. We met one of the bartenders last night while taking a walk, and he assured us he would serve us if we came back tonight. It's a Wednesday, and his boss won't show up until eleven." Kenzie's brown eyes sparkled with excitement.

Hannah didn't remember them going for a walk the night before. They must have left after she'd fallen asleep.

"Yeah, he is so hot," Jenny added, wiggling her brows.

"Are you sure you want to do that?" Cassidy asked, looking at Jenny.

It was odd that Cassidy had questioned her like that, but Jenny gave a small nod.

"Yes, we're sure," Kenzie snapped.

"Ugh, bars are not my thing. You guys know I don't like to drink. I will probably stay in and find a movie or something." She didn't want to be drinking to begin with, especially not in a foreign country.

"You will not," Kenzie snapped. She was the friend who always controlled what they each did, no matter what Hannah wanted.

Hannah needed to branch out from the friends she'd had in high school. She preferred to keep to herself, though, so making new friends was not very easy.

Cassidy grimaced at the tone of Kenzie's demand.

"I just don't think it will be my scene," Hannah said delicately.

"It will be evening when they open, so you won't have to be in the sun, and he said he would get us cheap drinks. There are less people there on weeknights. Plus, with a holiday next week, we pretty much have this place to ourselves." Kenzie ticked off each of the items she considered to be benefits on her manicured nails. "Don't be such a stick-in-the-mud." Kenzie's pushiness was easily one of Hannah's least favorite of her traits.

Hannah ran her fingers through her hair. This was not what she wanted. Her idea of a good time was getting off the beach and going on some kind of excursion. She wanted adventure, not getting drunk at a beach cantina. Sighing internally, she resigned herself to the idea that she was doomed to tag along or listen to whining the rest of the day. "Fine, I will go for an hour."

A triumphant smile spread across Kenzie's lips, making Hannah figure she was already plotting how to force her into staying for the entire evening. Hannah intended to remain firm on her time. She deserved to have what she wanted on this trip too.

Sick of sitting in her chair, she pulled on her hat. Sunburns on the scalp were the worst. She would look and feel like a molting snake for weeks as the burned skin flaked off.

Each step through the sand burned her feet. "Should have put on my flip-flops," she muttered to herself. Reaching the edge of the damp sand, she was glad to find the relief of the cool ocean water on her toes. Settling into the sand, she sat close enough to the edge to keep her toes in the waves' path. Each time the water receded, she felt like something she desperately wanted was taken away from her. Again.

When there was only an hour left until the cantina opened, they returned to their room to get ready for the evening. Hannah was tossed a small blue dress. "You expect me to wear this?" She held the dress up against her front. If it covered her small figure, she would be surprised.

"Han, I wear that dress all the time. It will cover all your bits." Kenzie rolled her chocolate eyes as she pulled items from her suitcase haphazardly. The woman had packed enough clothes to spend a month in Mexico.

"I brought plenty of clothes," Hannah replied, aiming to toss the dress back at Kenzie. Perhaps at her face.

Kenzie scoffed, "You brought a bunch of shit my mom would wear. You brought a one-piece swimsuit."

Hannah dressed more modestly than the rest of her friends. She had packed T-shirts, tank tops, Bermuda shorts, and her apparently offensive swimsuit. "There is nothing wrong with my clothes." Hannah pulled her brows together in a frown.

"Han, for one night, dress like you're going somewhere other than to dinner with your grandma," Kenzie said, placing a hand on one jutted-out hip.

Knowing when to fight Kenzie and when not to was becoming more and more blurred. Rolling her eyes, Hannah took the too-small dress into the bathroom. Pulling the material down over her head and over her hips, she felt as if she were in a straitjacket. Every inch of skin the dress hugged emphasized the curves she didn't have. The deep V-neck had her pulling the fabric at the edges closer together, trying to cover as much of herself as possible. Tugging the hem as low as she could, she checked herself in the mirror. She was relieved to see the material covered her rear. She was the most petite of their group. If this dress fit Kenzie, she knew it must be difficult for her to keep the fabric covering everything. She hated to admit it, but the color showed off the brilliance of her eyes.

Smoothing the material out one last time, she joined the others in their living room. Each was sporting a tight-fitting dress that left little to the imagination. Hannah and Cassidy were the only two who weren't comfortable with tight, flashy clothing. Meeting Cassidy's gaze, she knew she was just as uncomfortable. The flush in her cheeks was from more than just the sun, and she kept tugging at the bottom of the sage-green dress. It looked great with her dark skin and curls.

"We'll leave after an hour," Hannah whispered to Cassidy as they grabbed their purses.

Cassidy gave her a half smile then shifted her gaze to the other girls.

"Let's go, bitches," Jenny shouted, raising her arms above her head as she exited their room.

Cassidy gave Jenny a strange look. Before Hannah had a chance to question it, Kenzie screamed in agreement while Cassidy and Hannah shared another look of discomfort. Hannah linked her arm with Cassidy's. Cassidy squeezed hers back in return. They would be one another's life preservers.

The cantina was lit up with twinkle lights, and the young man behind the bar had short, dark hair. He was tan and lean. Hannah could see his appeal. She didn't feel entirely at ease with the idea of drinking in a foreign country, though. It was only Mexico, but she knew how crazy her friends could get when they drank too much. Hannah checked her phone. Time starts now.

Kenzie pointed to a small table that would accommodate all four of them and slid off her shoes to walk through the sand. The others followed suit.

Once seated, Hannah ordered a spiked seltzer, and Cassidy selected the same, while Jenny and Kenzie ordered mixed drinks. The bartender went heavy on the liquor, but he had a generous smile that put her defenses on edge. It was likely just the thought of her recent ex-boyfriend that made her judge him so harshly. He had a similar easy smile, given to anyone who looked his way. It was what drew her to him.

Returning to their table, the girls discussed their impending departure. Jenny and Kenzie were clearly displeased with the thought. Hannah hoped Cassidy shared in her sense of relief. Two more days.

Hannah sipped her drink slowly while Kenzie and Jenny went up for refills. Jenny's long brown ponytail swayed as she walked.

"I get a bad feeling from him," Cassidy whispered, eyeing the bartender wearily. Her deep-brown eyes narrowed.

"I thought that was just me." Hannah watched his movements. He was very fluid and caused the others to "oooh" and "ahh" over his bottle-flipping tricks. She wanted to see him do something to warrant her anxiety. Nothing. She was trying to tell herself she was being foolish, but something niggled in her mind.

The hairs on the back of her neck stood at attention, as if someone were breathing on the delicate skin. Turning over her shoulder, she saw nothing other than two men lounging on the beach, each with a beer in his hand. They paid her group no attention. No quick glances, nothing.

The sound of several glasses hitting the tabletop brought Hannah back around. Kenzie and Jenny returned with their mixed drinks and four shots.

"What are those?" Cassidy asked with an irritated huff.

"Tequila." Jenny shimmied her large breasts back and forth. Although she was the next shortest of their group, she was the curviest. Regardless of the hair tie she'd used to pull it back out of her face, her neverendingly straight hair swirled around her face as the winds picked up.

"No." Cassidy wrinkled her nose.

"Yes, Carter actually suggested it." Hannah swore she heard Kenzie swoon when she said his name. Another reason for Kenzie to want to extend their trip.

Hannah wrinkled her nose at the shot glass in front of her, and she wanted to swat it away. But her peacekeeping tendencies prevented disaster. Instead, she lifted the glass, looking to Cassidy, who was the only one not raising a glass.

"One," Cassidy hissed at the others. She hated drinking, and they all knew it. With multiple alcoholics in her family, Cassidy refused to let herself become like them.

"To Carter," Kenzie purred.

Hannah checked her phone. She didn't want to toast to the bartender, but the hour would be up in only another thirty minutes. She took the shot, and the liquor burned her throat, slithering through her veins, sinking its fangs into the depths of her middle. It seeped into her muscles faster than anything she'd ever had. The movements around her were suddenly going at hyperspeed, and she couldn't force her eyes or her mind to keep up with their actions.

She rarely drank, but this was a different sensation, like trying to run through waist-deep water. She blinked several times to bring her vision back into focus. Training her eyes on Jenny's lips, she tried to concentrate on what she was saying. It was as if she were talking with her hand over her mouth. Hannah leaned in closer, straining her ears to hear better. Shifting her gaze to Cassidy, she found her swaying slightly from side to side, a dazed expression filling her features. Something was wrong.

Ice-cold panic raced through Hannah's veins as she looked up at Carter. He was looking at them with a cool smile as he made his way around the bar, heading straight for them. Hannah tried to force herself to sober up. These next moments would be critical.

"Girls, I think we need to go back to the room." Her voice shook with fear as it raced through her. "Kenzie, did you pay for everything already?" She prayed the answer would be yes, but knowing Kenzie, she would have started a tab.

"I'm not leaving." Her words were slurred as she clung to

Jenny's drooping shoulders. They both looked worse off than she felt. They appeared as though they would collapse at any moment.

"I think there was something in those shots. Look at us." Hannah's voice sounded foreign to her own ears. It was louder than usual. The shrill sound made the hairs on the back of her neck prickle again.

"Stop, Han," Kenzie sneered, rolling her eyes at Hannah. "Just because Jackson treated you like shit doesn't mean all men are out to get you."

Jenny burst into laughter, and Hannah was shocked by both their outbursts. She hated the thoughts coursing through her. *Could my friends have been part of this plan? Would they try to hurt me?* That was all the more reason for her to get out of there.

"This has nothing to do with Jackson and his cheating ass." She implored the others, hoping they would realize the danger they could be in.

Cassidy looked ill, swaying in her chair.

"Cassidy, are you okay?" Hannah held on to her arm.

"I feel too drunk. I only had two." Cassidy's brows furrowed. "Not even. I didn't finish my seltzer."

Hannah saw her own confusion mirrored on her best friend's face.

The more Hannah tried to reach sobriety, the quicker she felt it slipping away. Her head was spinning on a Tilt-a-Whirl—everything was moving too fast and at odd angles. Hannah worried she was going to be sick.

"We need to go back to the room." She pulled on Cassidy's arm, determined to get at least one person back to their room before things got worse.

"Party poopers," Jenny slurred at their backs, giggling.

Hannah practically dragged Cassidy across the sand. Cassidy was slender but taller than Hannah, making them stumble as they went. Arm wrapped around her friend's back, Hannah could feel herself slipping farther into an abyss she knew she couldn't succumb to. She blinked faster, trying to fight away the exhaustion threatening to overtake her.

Cassidy's movements were equally clumsy as they moved across the sand.

"Han, I can't do this." Cassidy tripped, almost bringing them both to the ground.

Hannah's heart jumped into her throat, elevating the fear.

"Yes, you can. We have to." Hannah forced the words out. She was choking on the words she forced from her lips.

The sand pulled them back as they struggled forward. It might as well have been quicksand. Hannah was sinking into the depths of an impossible haze faster than she could place one heavy foot in front of the other. Her group and the two men had remained the only people on the beach near the cantina. She saw no resort staff anywhere.

She chanced a glance over her shoulder. The bartender was at the table with Jenny and Kenzie. She wanted to shout at him, to tell him to get away from them. She couldn't make a sound. Her breathing was labored, and words were impossible to form. No sound would cross her lips. The only sound she heard was her heart beating out of her chest. She felt each pulse throughout her body.

She wondered if her exertion was making things worse. Focusing back on the hotel, she pushed on as a burning filled her lungs. Then something was pressing on her hips, restricting movement. Each of her movements felt like they were disjointed and erratic. Her heart was beating in an irregular pattern. She held a hand to her chest to calm it. It felt as if it were bouncing off her ribs like a ping-pong ball.

"Calling it a night?" one of the men from the beach asked. Hannah didn't like his tone.

"Just using the bathroom," she lied as she tried to propel Cassidy onto the small patio at the back door of the resort.

"Aw, don't lie to us, sweetheart," the bigger of the two men cooed.

She fought to swallow the lump forming in her throat. There was little she could do to avoid these men. Each step made her feel like there were bricks strapped to the bottoms of her feet. Her vision began to blur.

"I'll help you," the man said with a sadistic smirk, catching her arm in his grasp.

She tried to scream, but she couldn't. The darkness at her periphery was taking over all her senses. She was falling asleep. No, she was passing out. This wasn't as natural as sleep. This was something different. Something deadly.

The last thing she saw was the other man catching Cassidy before she fell onto the tan pavers before them. They'd almost made it. A single tear fell as she closed her eyes.

CHAPTER THREE
MARIA, JULY 2ND

"Great idea, Maria, to go on a road trip alone," she mocked herself as she pulled into one of the parking spaces outside the motel with the horrendous pink sign. The small motel was on the outskirts of town and looked a little worse for wear. The building was a bland shade of tan, much like the others in the area. Tan and pale yellow seemed to be the go-to colors. The parking lot had large cracks with small vegetation struggling to take hold and survive in the New Mexico heat. The motel itself was in the shape of a horseshoe, with the parking lot in the center.

The motel was nothing to brag about, but it would beat sleeping in her car again. Maria rolled her head around her shoulders, stretching the muscles and attempting to alleviate the pain and kinks from the long drive. She was exhausted. Maybe tomorrow would be a day of doing nothing other than wandering around Las Cruces. There was an art museum and a natural science museum—easy places to wander around for a few hours. Both were places she knew she could lose herself in. The emotions. The wonders.

Pulling her purse over her shoulder, she made her way to what she could only assume was the office. The section to the right of the horseshoe was nearly all windows. It looked like the nicest part of the building's façade. As she stepped into the room, a bell chimed, and the stench of body odor and cigarettes slapped her in the face. Great. She hoped the rest of the place had a better aroma.

A tall, thin man emerged from a doorway behind the front desk. His eyes narrowed on her as if she were trespassing.

"Hi. Can I get a room?" she asked, knowing the exhaustion she felt was etched into her features. Sleep was what she needed.

The man shifted nervously from one foot to the other.

She couldn't help the irritation that rushed through her.

"Did you reserve a room?"

"No. That's why I just asked if I could get a room." Her words had come out a bit more rude than she'd intended.

"I don't think we have any rooms available," he said, his small, beady black eyes shifting between her and the door.

Scoffing, she crossed her arms over her chest. "You're kidding, right? There are literally three cars in the parking lot, and you expect me to believe there are no rooms available?" So sleep-deprived Maria can be forceful, she mentally chastised herself. Not work Maria, though.

"There are other hotels in town."

"No, I'm here. I want a room. My brother owns this dump. Do you need me to call him to make sure I can get a damn room?"

His Adam's apple bobbed as he swallowed.

She knew now she was being extremely rude. She hated when people tried to play the I-know-someone-important card. But she got grumpy when she was tired, and this poor kid had met her on one of her worst days.

"Look, ma'am, I, ah, can't check you in tonight."

"And why not? I'm here. I'm a paying customer. I just need a place to sleep tonight. Give me a room, or I will be calling Patrick. This is ridiculous." As she reached for her phone, the clerk began to nod.

"Okay, okay." He wiped away the sweat gathering on his forehead beneath his dark, scraggly hair.

For what felt like an eternity, she watched the man as he punched keys frantically on the computer. He looked older than she had estimated when she first arrived. Telltale signs of age jumped out at her, from the lines creasing the corners of his eyes to the white hairs sprinkled throughout his dark scruff.

"Here's your key. Room six." He pointed to the right of where they stood. Taking the ancient-looking key from him, she was surprised it was an actual metal key with a pink ribbon dangling from it, not a key card.

After retrieving her bags from her car, she made her way to the door with a golden number six on it. The room smelled only marginally better than the lobby. Although it didn't smell of cigarettes, it still had the musty stench of sweat. Maria trudged over to the bed and pulled back the covers. She could smell the pungent odor of bleach, so they had been cleaned. But apparently, the bedsheets were so old, even bleach couldn't keep them white.

The entire room made her stomach roil with intense disgust. She'd never visited Las Cruces despite her brother owning this motel. Standing in it now, she didn't think it was much to speak of. The carpet was old and fraying at some of the seams. The walls were painted a horrendous shade of baby vomit.

This is not the Ritz, she thought to herself, throwing the covers back into place and curling her upper lip at the old coverings. To think, I was worried the clerk wasn't going to let me check in. She could always get the picnic blanket she carried in her car. It was a warm night, so she could sleep on top of the covers. Minimum contact would be best for her peace of mind.

Pulling her phone from her pocket, she noticed a few notifications she didn't feel like addressing—two texts from Kameron, one from her mom, and one from the HR department at work. Ignoring the mocking envelope at the top of the screen, she checked how she was making out on her trip. The application she was using to track her progress showed all the roads she'd already traveled. The small red line with its erratic design was not as long as she thought it should be. Two days of driving for several hours should have added up to more distance. Sighing, she tossed her phone down on the dressing table, and it landed with a dull thud.

Looking at the lit screen, she felt guilty for not responding to Kameron. They'd met in kindergarten and had been inseparable for years. Then Kameron had moved across the state, and they'd lost contact until high school. Social media. It's amazing who I could find when I looked hard enough.

The messages were likely Kameron apologizing again, especially with all that Maria had going on. Without Kameron sharing the expenses, Maria had needed to make sacrifices and sleep in her car the night before. No matter the cost, she would not be doing that again.

With a groan of self-pity, she began looking around at the small room—she was regretting traveling alone. The hours in the car were long and lonely. She could only sing along to her favorite songs so many times before they became mundane.

Looking out the small window beside the door, she noticed a few cars in the parking lot below the motel's neon road sign. The Roadrunner Motel—she'd always thought it was an odd name. Earlier, she'd thought the empty lot was a good sign, but now, she figured it was due to the poor quality of the motel itself and the way the employees treated guests. An anxious warning filled her belly. She studied the front-desk clerk as he made his way down the front of the motel. He was going from room to room with a rubbish cart. He spent only a moment or two beyond the threshold before returning to the cart and depositing something onto the shelves. He was just nearly around the bend, walking away from her. It was odd.

She closed the curtains against the neon sign, but the outline of the aggressive pink light was still visible through the old black curtains. Turning back to her room, she pulled her bedclothes from her bag. Her shirt was damp with perspiration—the hot days were wearing on her.

Venturing into the small bathroom, she reminded herself this was exactly why she preferred the East Coast. The winters were cold, but she would take the snow over unbearable heat any day. On a snowy day, she could cover up with a fuzzy blanket and get lost in a movie. She peeled her shirt over her head. Disgusted by the dampness, she tossed both the shirt and her bra into the plastic bag she'd brought for dirty clothes.

The shower was small and stained, and the showerhead sat low on the wall. The height wasn't an issue for her, as she was barely five and a half feet tall on her best days, with a little help from her preferred clogs. Using the provided soaps, she cleaned herself up, washing away the sweat caked to her skin and the irritation directed at Kameron that she didn't deserve. She'd canceled because she was covering for someone who was seriously ill at work.

Wishing she didn't have to come to a life-altering decision at the end of this trip, Maria rubbed her temples. She tried to force the nagging thoughts to dissipate. She would think about it long and hard tomorrow. Today, she would relax the rest of the day. After all, she had four more days.

After showering, she dressed in a lightweight tank top and shorts then retrieved the grass-stained picnic blanket from the trunk of her car. She settled down onto the blanket atop the bed. Lying down felt good, so long as she didn't think too hard about what she might be lying on. She needed the rest. Falling asleep was easier than she'd initially anticipated.

Startled awake, dazed, she sat upright. Listening and concentrating on her surroundings, she tried to pinpoint the direction of the noise. Turning her head from side to side, she could hear whimpering or crying next door. She pressed her ear to the wall, but the sounds quickly moved away. The alarm clock on the nightstand showed it was almost eleven. She groped in the dark for her cell phone.

She heard moaning. Is someone hurt? She strained her ears. Silence. Then there was movement outside her door. She froze with fear. On instinct, she slowed her breathing, while her heart kicked into overdrive. She needed to focus on the sounds beyond her door. Maybe the girl she'd heard was going for a walk.

There was more shuffling. That's too much noise for one person.

The door to her room swung open and bounced off the opposite wall with a resounding bang. Two large figures stood in the doorway. Two things registered. First, neither was the woman Maria thought she'd heard. Second, her phone was still on the dressing table, which was closer to them than to her.

"Why is she awake?" one of the figures barked at the other.

"How am I supposed to know? I got here same time you did."

They exchanged a look and proceeded into her room. It was too dark for her to make out their faces. Still trying to figure out her best option, she scrambled out of the bed, ran to the far window, and threw open the curtains. Fumbling with the latch on the window, she heard them approaching her quickly. This was it. There was nothing she could do.

That wasn't true—she could fight. Spinning around, she found herself practically nose to chest with one of the men. Shoving off his chest, she tried to run around him. He didn't budge. His reflexes were quick. He had a fistful of her hair before she could take three steps away from him.

"Just where do ya think ya goin', sweetheart? Ya' comin' with us," he said with a false sweetness to his voice.

She shivered at the sound of his words.

A large tattooed arm wrapped around her front and pinned both her arms to her sides. His hand wrapped all the way around her upper arm. She kicked and wriggled as much as she could. Her feet connected with his shins, but he didn't react.

"Don' jus' stand there like a damn idiot," he cursed at his cohort. When the other man still looked confused, he barked, "Grab her fuckin' legs." Still holding her hair in his other hand, he pulled her head as far back as he could, so she was no longer able to see anything but his chin. The dark, coarse stubble brushed her temple as he spoke. "Ya make a sound, and I will snap ya damn neck."

Before she could formulate a retort, the second man pinned her legs together. He was smaller than the first, older too. In her peripheral vision, she could see he had white or gray hair. It was hard to tell in the partial darkness. The only light in the room came from the streetlights and the motel sign.

Another man entered the room. "What the hell are you doing in this room?" There was something slightly familiar about his voice. *Where have I heard it before?*

Unable to see anything other than the first man's hard-set jaw, she believed he would indeed break her neck if she so much as squeaked. The panic taking up residence in her throat likely wouldn't allow her to speak even if she wanted to.

"You missed one on your rounds," the second man stated angrily.

Rounds? What could that possibly mean?

Before she had time to ponder it, she heard the third man cross the room and caught his scraggly dingy-brown hair from the corner of her eye. The front-desk clerk. *That's why his voice sounded familiar.*

"Fuck," he said nervously. "She's not one of them. I told you guys it was only those four rooms." He pointed to the wall she'd just had her ear pressed up against.

"Then who the fuck is this?" the large man asked, shaking Maria. His grip on her arm intensified.

"She demanded to be checked in. Said there was no way there weren't any open rooms. She was persistent, kept sayin—"

The man holding her hair cut him off before he could finish. "I don' give a shit what she said. It's too late. You got any more doses left? She'll fit right in," he said with a sadistic smile.

"Man, you don't under—"

"Shut the fuck up, new kid. It's too damn late!" the large man barked as the front-desk clerk scampered off.

"Please, I won't say anything to anyone," she lied.

The clerk's hair rustled back and forth as he looked between the two men holding Maria.

"Nah, sweetheart. We're goin' to have a bit of fun."

Maria struggled against his hold, but he only gripped her harder, like a determined shark. With one quick shake, he could snap her neck.

"I don't have much left. This is only a partial."

Struggling to turn and see what he was referring to, she found her attempts were futile. The attempted movement caused tears to flood her eyes as his unrelenting grip ripped hairs from her scalp.

She felt a pinch, then a warming sensation flowed through her arm. Within seconds, the fight went out of her. She felt the hand on her hair relax, her head lolled to one side, and she saw the clerk. He looked terrified. *What does he have to fear? He isn't being kidnapped.*

"What is that squeaking sound?" When she didn't get a reply, she opened her eyes. Her surroundings were unfamiliar, and her vision was blurred. *What are all the sounds?*

Something was squeaking consistently. There was a rattling, almost like a chain was shaking, along with a steady hum.

Sitting up, she felt a sharp poke on the palms of her hands. Looking down, she was shocked to find hay scratching at her bare legs. Blinking her eyes into focus, she registered that she was moving a moment too late. She was thrown forward, landing hard on her forearms.

This time, when she sat up, she felt something soft under her fingers. A chill ran through her entire body. There was another girl lying in the hay. She was asleep—or unconscious. Probably drugged.

Her throat felt dry. The urge to scream conflicted with the dryness, and no one would hear the hoarse noises emanating from her lungs. Her heart hammered against her ribs as her palms became slick with her terror.

Desperate, she did her best to focus her vision on her surroundings. They were in some kind of trailer. There was nothing to grip to pull herself up to stand. Scooting herself over to one side, she struggled to maneuver around the other woman, trying to keep some space between them as she made her way to the wall. She didn't want to fall on the girl. It wasn't smooth, but the ridges and bumps in the metal gave her nothing to grip.

Another bump sent her head into the side of the trailer as she fell to her knees. "Damn it." She swore under her breath, holding her head between her hands. Giving herself a moment to collect herself, she nursed the pain in her head. Sticky warm blood coated her fingers. Pushing her auburn hair out of her face, she wiped the blood on her shorts. The silky material did little to absorb the smears.

Taking a deep breath, she pushed herself up to standing. Spreading her bare feet wide, she felt the stabbing pinch of the straw in the sensitive skin. She turned, cataloging everything she saw. Four other women lay in the hay. She'd seen the clerk visit four rooms.

Her breaths were coming in rapid succession. She didn't feel like she was taking in enough oxygen to process what was surrounding her. She had to calm the shaky breaths. These girls looked so young. She doubted any of them were over the age of twenty-five. All were lying perfectly still.

The hand supporting her against the wall turned cold and clammy. Perspiration coated her skin like an icy cloak. What could these men possibly want with so many women? The possibilities rolled like boulders around her brain, each one worse than the one before, and colliding with one another with each disturbing thought.

Tears flowing, she dropped back down to her knees then crawled to the closest girl. Beautiful blond hair lay intermingled with the floor covering. Extending a shaky hand, she checked for a pulse. It was there and beating steadily. The girl was wearing a skimpy dress.

What if she had been on a date with one of these men? What if she was at a club and was taken? Maria hated to think of the possibilities.

Maria patted her down, checking her for pockets or anything useful. After finding nothing, she moved to the next girl, who was also wearing a small dress. She found no pockets on her either. The similar dresses made her suspect they'd been taken together. She approached the third woman, and each beat of her pulse gave Maria hope that they would all be okay in the end. Tears were still flowing down her cheeks. She didn't know how she was going to get them all out of this, but she had to try. First things first. She was going to make sure they were all okay—in the most basic sense of the word.

She scooted over to the girl with long dark, silky hair. Pressing her index and middle fingers to her neck, she felt for a pulse. Another bump in the road propelled Maria forward. She landed hard on her right hand. Cursing, she sat back up and replaced her fingers on the girl's neck.

Letting out a strangled cry, she pressed more firmly. Fingers shaking frantically, she felt around. Nothing. The girl's skin was barely warm to the touch.

She lowered her head to place her ear just above the girl's mouth and nose. Other than the sounds of the tires and general jostling of the trailer, she could hear nothing. She felt nothing. No warm, damp breath disturbed Maria's hair that fell over the girl's face.

Tears were stinging her eyes and blurring her vision. This is not happening. They're all going to be okay. How could this be? Her hands shook more than she would ever be able to control. She needed to be steady, as levelheaded as possible.

"Take a breath," she told herself.

Knowing her panic would only make the situation worse, she forced herself to sit back up and take a few deep breaths. Resting her hand on the other woman's diaphragm, she tried to see if she could feel her move. Still nothing.

She had been trained in CPR years ago. Now was the test. Gently tipping the girl's head back, she pinched her nose and released her own breath over to the girl—willing her to accept it. She did the chest compressions, gave her another breath, more compressions. On and on. With each transferred breath, more hot tears fell from her burning eyes.

Nothing. She wanted to scream for the young life that was lost.

Replacing the girl's head in the original position, Maria adjusted her dark hair, laying it over her shoulder. She looked so sweet and innocent. Maria estimated she was likely in her late teens or early twenties. A child.

These men needed to pay. They'd stolen all their lives.

Forcing herself to continue, she checked on the remaining girl. She had thick black hair and dark skin. Holding her breath, Maria pressed her fingers into the girl's neck. She was alive, and Maria let out a strangled sigh of relief. Giving the tiny woman one last glance, she crawled to the back of the trailer, no longer noticing the pinpricks of the straw on her hands and knees. She didn't care. What did she have to complain about? She had a chance to get herself and the others out of this. And that was just what she planned to do.

Crawling over to where the doors should have been, she found her path blocked. Hay bales were stacked from floor to ceiling, barring anyone on the inside from the door. If she tried to move them, the only place she had to put them was on top of the others.

Bracing herself on the side of the trailer, she forced herself to her feet. She could see small narrow openings at the top of the trailer walls. Scrambling to the nearest opening, she tried to reach the cool night air. Being mindful of the girls around her, she jumped, stretching out her hands as high as she could. She got the fingertips of her right hand over the metal edge but lost her grip quickly. Each time she landed back in the trailer, her feet slipped and slid, while her brain felt as if it were rolling from side to side. The trauma of hitting her head before was rearing its disastrous consequences, but she couldn't give up. No, a headache is not going to stop me.

If someone driving by saw her hand through that window, they would have a chance for survival. This could save them all—well, the rest of them.

After several minutes of trying to hold herself up, she was finally able to hold on but only by her fingertips. It was impossible for her to hold up her entire weight with one hand in this way. As the truck hit another particularly large bump, she cried out in pain when her fingers let loose. The metal edge ripped at her nails.

She slammed down onto her knees and sat where she'd landed, sobs racking her body. Consumed by exhaustion, she turned so her back was braced on the side of the trailer. The cold metal pressed into her spine. Allowing her head to hang, she laid her forearms over her bent knees.

"What am I to do?" she whispered. She didn't want to give up, but she also knew exerting more energy would be useless. She didn't have the fight or emotional stability to continue struggling tonight. Her head was getting worse, causing her vision to blur. There was nothing she could do at the moment. She had to wait. She needed to conserve what little energy she had remaining.

Looking up, she figured she had been awake for a couple hours. The sun should be coming up soon. She promised herself that when the truck stopped, she would try something, anything. She needed to make contact with her brother. What would he say about the women staying in his motel being kidnapped?

The more she thought about it, the stranger it seemed.

She lost the fight against unconsciousness. Lying down between the other girls, she succumbed to the fatigue. More hot tears slid down her face. Each time she closed her eyes, she saw the two large men barging into her motel room. When she didn't dream of them, she dreamed of what might await when the truck stopped. Each time she awoke, the anxiety in her middle grew. The danger of getting sick increased with each minute. Images of more needles, merciless criminals, and the other girls filled her mind. The restless sleep would do little to help her think clearly. Nevertheless, she reminded herself she needed to do what she could.

CHAPTER FOUR
PATRICK, JULY 2ND

"Thanks for the update, Grant." Patrick slammed the phone back into the cradle. He flexed his hands, releasing the anger festering in the joints. The urge to punch something—or better yet, someone—was hard to ignore.

Running a hand through his thick, dark hair, he pulled at the ends, causing them to stand up at odd angles. Releasing a pent-up breath, he pushed away from his desk. His office sat above what used to be a movie theater. Windows were positioned to allow him to see everything happening in the theater below. It was getting prepped for the new shipment.

Boxes were being erected because some of the new customers were worried about being recognized. He tracked everything from what they drove into his parking lot to their most recent outings. No one was invited to be part of his auctions unless they were able to pay the price and keep their mouth shut.

Patrick was worried that the young man he'd hired for the motel was incompetent. There were strict rules—no vacancies and no check-ins on delivery days. The rules were simple, and he was paid well for the little he did. The little shit couldn't even keep that straight, though. Maybe he didn't value his daughter's life as much as he'd said. Patrick would need to speak with him before the next stopover.

As if sensing his need for a distraction, Veronica barged into his office. She was always good for some kind of simple tragedy that could be fixed in a matter of minutes. She was the only person who could walk into his office unannounced. She was the first woman he'd hired and the only person he trusted completely. There were men that did the runs he felt he could trust more than most, but he still questioned each of them at times. Suspicion kept him vigilant.

"I'm worried about the new hairdresser you brought on." She snapped her gum as she spoke.

"What's wrong with her?" He let his irritation seep into the question.

She eyed him slowly then surged forward. "She's late every day. She has no sense of style." Veronica ticked off each of the girl's faults with a long-manicured finger. "She can't cut hair to save her life. She..."

"Okay, okay, I get it." Patrick put his hands in the air in surrender. "For fuck's sake, give her one week styling the girls. She's stuck here and can't really go anywhere else."

Sabrina had an unappeasable drug problem, and she'd found her way into Patrick's building when he was feeling particularly generous. So he'd made a deal with her. He compensated her so she could keep up with her fixes, and she guaranteed she wouldn't run to the police. Club Phoenix served multiple purposes. It was a strip club on most nights, and he liked to make sure his dancers were done up well. That included having a hairdresser.

Veronica brought everything to him, even after she solved things on her own. She made sure he was in the know. The men on the runs didn't tell him everything, though. Installing cameras at each of his locations had been on his mind for months. Perhaps it was getting to be time to do so. More cameras meant more evidence, though.

Jutting out one of her hips, Veronica placed her taloned hand on the distended bone. She was thin to the extreme. Surprisingly, she'd never touched drugs. Being slender was her only goal in life—and that was likely the real reason Veronica didn't like Sabrina. Veronica was predictable. That was just what Patrick liked about her. It kept her constant.

He usually only got complaints from Veronica, and she was in a class all by herself. She had a thing for designer clothes to hang off her skin-and-bone frame. She would do anything he asked of her even if she complained about it at first.

There were always certain people who needed slightly different motivators. Patrick had a knack for figuring out what those particular motivators were and how to use them to his advantage.

"What?" He intensified his scowl, hoping she would leave him to fester in his anger alone.

With a shrug, she left the office, her curly dirty-blond hair swishing behind her.

"Finally," he muttered, dropping back into his chair. The anger he wanted to wallow in was no longer within reach, though.

Glaring at his phone, he watched as it rang again. This time, it was Sam, checking in right on time. With a groan, he answered.

"Eagle Warehouse is ready. There are four beds set up and waiting."

Patrick contemplated telling Sam about the surprise additional guest who was on the way. But he wanted to see how the men at the warehouse were going to respond and how long it would take them to tell him about the mix-up at the motel. This was to be the test of their reliability.

"Thanks, Sam."

Patrick listened as Sam droned on about what he'd done to get everything set up. Sam was a pleaser. He wanted gratitude and appreciation from everyone. He got annoying at moments like this, but as long as Patrick kept the call short, he would be able to escape the man's nonsensical jabbering.

"Thanks again, Sam. I've got a meeting." Hanging up, he rubbed his eyes with his thumb and index finger. He wondered if he'd been hiring a bunch of dumbasses. Capable and willing—that was all he needed. Simplicity was never what he got.

CHAPTER FIVE
MARIA, JULY 3RD

When the trailer stopped, Maria was startled awake. It was still dark and cold, which did not make any sense. She should have been able to see the sunshine through the openings above.

The doors to the truck opened and closed, but only two doors made a sound. Only two men were in the truck. The motel clerk must have stayed behind.

"Fastest drive we done so far, Grant." The man sounded happy with himself.

As silently as she could, she moved herself to the far end of the trailer. She settled down among the others so she might get a chance to see what was coming. She couldn't imagine she and the others would be left in the trailer. She took a steadying breath.

Maria heard several pairs of feet shuffling outside the trailer. Their footsteps echoed, making it difficult to figure out how many men were out there. Staying as still as she could, she tried to pick out what was being said.

"Count the cots and get them out of the trailer. We will need to get them changed and hooked up before we can leave again." The man's voice paused for a moment.

Everyone was silent. This must be their boss. Maria strained with everything in her body to hear what was going on. The other women's breathing made it difficult to hear. She couldn't allow herself to be annoyed by such an essential and comforting sound. She stole a glance at the young woman who could no longer breathe. Maria didn't know the girl's name, but she was sickened to think of how the last few hours of her life must have played out. The fear she must have felt.

"We will need to have them each given a dosage at six o'clock," the same stern voice advised.

The latch on the trailer screeched as it slid out of the way. It made her want to cover her ears to protect them from the assaulting sound. With the door open, a small amount of light trickled in through the opening as the hay bales were removed from the doorway. They were stacked three deep and were removed one by one. With each bale, more light was let in, and the more hope she felt.

Watching through her lashes, Maria saw the outline of two men. One looked like the smaller of the two from the motel room. The second was of a similar size, yet he appeared to be decades older, wearing glasses. They were silent as they went about their work.

They stacked the bales of hay just beyond the door of the trailer. Lying in the back proved to be problematic. She couldn't see over the girls in front of her, and she wondered if the men would notice she was not where they had placed her the night before. Panic began creeping through her body. Her heart was racing, and she worried it would be loud enough for someone else to hear too. The thoughts of being removed from the trailer were comforting for a moment, but now she was terrified by what she would find on the other side of the metal walls surrounding her. Her prison also gave her protection.

With the bales out of the way, three men entered and began lifting the girls. One of the large men was the one who'd grabbed her the night before. She watched as they lifted each limp body into their arms. Self-preservation prevented her from losing it right then and there. She hated them touching the girls. She wanted to shout at them, to scream for help.

The men were working silently, and so far, there were at least four men. The odds were not in her favor. There was no way she would be able to get past them all.

The trailer shook as a man made his way into the trailer. She did her best to stay still and pretend to be asleep. If this man couldn't hear her heart or her labored breathing, she would be stunned. He lifted her easily, one arm around her back with his hand resting on her ribcage just below her right breast. The other arm was under her knees, cradling her like a mother would her baby. She hated the feeling, but she forced her head and limbs to hang listlessly as they moved about. Her head bobbed and wiggled as he moved, and it was nauseating.

"One left." A man called from the opening of the trailer.

"That one takes the last cot," another voice chimed in.

"There were only supposed to be four!" the stern voice barked.

Even with her eyes closed, she could tell when they were no longer in the trailer. The light beyond her eyelids seemed brighter. The light was blocked as another of the men went back into the trailer. It took everything in her not to move.

His feet shuffled around in the trailer for a moment. "There's an issue in here."

The man dropped Maria onto a cot as her heart raced. She let her head fall to the side to keep the trailer in sight. The girl who didn't survive was the only one left. Now they knew—they knew they were murderers too.

The man's brow furrowed in what appeared to be disgust. "Dispose of her," the man said, showing no emotion for the girl. Heartless.

Maria forced herself to keep from clenching her hands into fists. Anger simmered in her veins.

"Grant, in my office," the man demanded.

Grant, the man who'd held her by her hair the night before, followed the man through a door to her feet. They were gone, and the other two were in the trailer, taking care of the girl. Sensing an opportunity, she slid one leg off the edge of the cot then waited to see if anyone noticed her. Shifting her other leg over, she sat up. The movement was too fast, and bile rose into her throat. As the queasiness subsided, the two men in the trailer emerged, and she lay back down just in time as one of them turned quickly in her direction—the second man from the motel room.

"C'mon, Ivan. I hate doing this shit," the shorter, older man said.

"This ain't my idea of a goddamn party either, Sam," Ivan spat as they carried the dead woman out the bay door.

This was it, her chance. Bringing her feet back to the floor, she sat up, more confident this time. The concrete was cold under her feet. She pushed up off the cot and staggered to the nearest wall. Muscles that she didn't know she had ached. The fatigue made her fall harder against the wall than she intended. The sound echoed off the corrugated walls. Her legs shook as she tried to force herself to run. But she felt as if she'd done leg day for the first time in years, and her body didn't know how to function anymore.

Gripping a two-by-four that made up the backbone of the walls, she pulled herself forward. The warehouse was small. It fit the trailer and the cots, and it looked as if it might have room for two more of those horse trailers. It was a small space, which was a relief. There was only one door, and it was now filled by the two figures who had taken the girl from the trailer.

"I told him," Ivan was saying as his cold eyes landed on Maria. They darkened when they met hers. "Sam," he said, nodding in Maria's direction.

The two men advanced into the room. Each of her steps was eaten up by two of theirs as she tried to turn and run the other way. Staggering, she stumbled forward as her knees buckled under her. A strong, tanned arm snaked around her waist.

"Get off me," she shouted, flailing her legs and arms. Bringing an elbow back as hard as she could, she tried to connect with his ribs. A sharp groan rushed across her neck, disturbing her hair and causing a shiver to run over her body.

"You bitch," he groaned. Kicking out one of his legs, he wrapped it around hers. Knocking her off her feet, he brought them both down to the ground, pressing her into the dirty concrete with his own body. "You're lucky I can't fuck up your face," Ivan whispered into her ear. His breath smelled of mints, and she was annoyed that it wasn't something off-putting. She wanted him to be as disgusting in all ways as he appeared by his actions.

To her right, the door to the office swung open, and Grant and the boss emerged.

"Up already?" the man asked, checking his watch. "Should have had another hour or so left."

"She got the partial dose," Grant said, crossing his tattooed arms across his broad chest. These men were built for cornering others. She was hardly made for running.

"Ahh, right. You see, you helped us out by demanding to be checked in. Now, we don't have to disappoint by reporting one dead. You will go in her place." His smile would have forced the joy out of the happiest of people.

"No, I won't," Maria said with as much force as she could muster.

"Oh, but you will, because if you don't, you'll be with her." The man hitched his thumb in the direction of the open bay door. The light breeze wafting in mocked her.

"Do you want me to shut that door, sir?" Sam asked. His glasses slid down his nose, and using his thumb, he pushed them back up.

Sir? None deserved the respect of that title. She wanted to tell him so, but enraging him would not be her best idea.

"Ivan, take her to get dressed first. If she fights, persuade her to cooperate."

The weight pressing Maria into the floor lifted, and Ivan dragged her to her feet.

"Back in a moment, Frank." The joy crossing Ivan's cold features froze her with fear. She didn't want to go anywhere alone with this man. But fighting him in front of everyone else would only prove she was a problem. She just needed to survive the day. They would be loaded back into the trailer tonight. During that transition, she would try something—anything.

Ivan kept a ruthless grip on her bicep as he led her to a door she hadn't noticed. When he pushed open the swinging door, she found herself in a single-occupancy restroom. A rolling rack stood in the corner, holding four velour track suits.

"Strip and put one of those on," Ivan demanded, hitching his chin at the rack in the corner. He leaned against the door as if he had not a worry in the world, as if this were an everyday occurrence. The lack of care in his dark eyes made her want to shiver.

Swallowing, Maria gaped at him. Her mouth fell open, but she couldn't force the words she wanted to say from her parted lips. She was already wearing little more than underwear.

"You have until I count to ten, and then I will be coming over there to help you." His eyes roved over her body. She wanted to cover herself, to shield her body from his firm gaze. "One... two..."

"Fine," Maria croaked. Tears filled her eyes again. She didn't want to find out how he would help her. Making her way over to the rack, she turned her back to him. She let her silky shorts fall to the floor as she pulled one of the suits from the rack. Jerking the pants up to her hips, she was grateful she'd worn underwear to bed. Far too often, she slept in just her shorts. She reached behind her for a top and pulled the zip-up hoodie on over her tank.

"Done. Can I have some privacy to use the toilet?" She tried and failed to keep her anger at bay.

Chapter Six
Hannah, July 3rd

Hannah tried to open her heavy eyelids. The task sounded so simple, but it was impossible. She couldn't lift her lashes. It was as if they were glued down. She moved her eyeballs from side to side. It felt as if there was sand inside her eyelids. She groaned at the slicing feeling.

"Is another one waking up?" a gruff voice asked.

She knew she'd heard that voice before, but it wasn't someone she knew. Concentrating on where she'd heard the voice, she remembered the strange motel from the night before. Realization dropped on her like the rain of a torrential downpour. She'd almost woken up when someone took her out of bed. Fear raced through her body. Something scraped across the floor. It must have been a chair. But try as she might, she still couldn't move anything.

She tried to swallow as she thought of what might be coming. Her limbs were numb. She tried to wiggle her fingers or her toes. Sense was telling her it was best to keep still, but her panic told her she needed to move. She needed to escape.

More movement around the room let her know there was at least one other person in the room. She was terrified to think of what was going to happen to her. A tear slid free as she thought of

Cassidy. Hannah hoped she was okay. What kind of friend did that make her if Cassidy was her first and only thought?

"I don't see anyone moving," a different voice said as the sound of more shuffling met her ears. Someone was close. Something brushed against her hand where it hung. At that moment, she realized she was lying on something. It was stiff.

She felt her other senses returning slowly. She closed her left hand into a fist. Her brain began to process more of the sounds around her. There were more people in the room. There was breathing from more than just the two men.

"I'll take the next one to get changed." The excitement in the man's voice told her this was nothing she wanted to do.

Pretending to remain asleep and wanting to run warred within her.

"What time do we give them the next dose?" the unfamiliar voice asked.

"Will ya calm down? This ain't my first time. Fuckin' Frank already said." More footsteps told her he was on the move. His voice was closer and laced with irritation. "Six for those three. Seven for that one. Then they be all set for the night."

Hannah concentrated on keeping her breathing even. *So there's four of us. Does that mean the others are with me?*

A small feminine groan filled the quiet.

"Which one?" This man was clearly nervous. Steps were farther away than before, frantic and scuffling around.

Finally able to lift her eyelids, she peered through her thin blond lashes. Kenzie lay on a cot to her right. She couldn't see any farther without moving her head. Two men stood over another cot at Kenzie's feet. She couldn't see who was on the other cot. Their backs were to her as she chanced a look down to her feet. A woman she didn't recognize sat upon the cot at her feet. Her hands were bound together, but she was awake and watching everything. A curtain of auburn hair blocked her face from Hannah's view. But it was easy to tell she was not one of Hannah's friends. That meant someone was missing. She stifled the cry that almost careened from her soul.

Movement from the men's direction had her settling back into place. Her pulse was thrumming quickly in her throat. She kept her eyes nearly shut, opening them just enough to peer between the gaps in her lashes.

"Do we get her changed now?" the nervous man asked. The pitch in his voice seemed to get higher each time he spoke.

"Why the fuck are ya here if ya can't handle shit?" the largest man growled.

The small man with glasses looked around as if someone might sneak up on him. "I didn't want to do this shit. I was forced into this position," he squeaked.

"If ya fuck this up for me, I'll kill ya."

The large man was looming over the other. The smaller man's shoulders shook with fear, and the anger radiating through the larger man was evident. This man was quick to flip and clearly dangerous. He was unpredictable.

Hate and fear of these men flamed her panic, increasing her already-thrumming heartrate. There was likely nothing she could do. The only things she'd dared to move were her eyes, head, and the hand dangling over the edge of her resting place. She was afraid that if she stood, her legs wouldn't be able to carry her. Every muscle in her body felt depleted.

The larger man shoved the other away from him. "Get ya shit together." He pointed an angry finger at the smaller, older man.

The old man had to push his glasses back up the bridge of his nose multiple times during their conversation.

Hannah heard another small groan, and this time, she recognized it as Cassidy. The urge to jump to her friend's aid was painful to suppress. The men moved over to her, forgetting their argument.

"Watch her," the large man growled.

The woman on the cot at Hannah's feet shifted forward, as if she, too, wished to lunge at these men, but her bound hands were strapped to the underside of her cot. If she tried to stand, she would faceplant.

A door squeaked open and slammed closed. The large man was gone, leaving just the smaller man. This could be her only chance. She swung one of her arms over herself, using the momentum to force herself to roll. She needed to stand—the floor was closer than she anticipated as her feet slammed down. She stumbled, and the muscles in her legs acted as if they no longer knew how to carry her. Her muscles felt like Jell-O. The man turned at the sound, and his wide eyes darted from her back down to Cassidy.

The other woman looked up at her, sadness etched into her features. Tape covered her mouth. There was too much to process. Jenny was missing. Her mind was spinning.

The man's closeness to Cassidy made Hannah's protective instincts jump to attention. Her jellied legs carried her clumsily between their makeshift beds. Before she could reach out to Cassidy, a large, rough hand closed tightly around her upper arm. Her balance was thrown off, and she fell back against the chest of another large man she hadn't noticed before. She had no idea if she'd ever seen such uncaring, harsh eyes. Everything that had happened before this moment felt like a lifetime ago.

"I guess we have a volunteer to go next, Grant," the man called.

Grant, the man who'd been talking with the older man, reentered the room. The woman on the cot was struggling against her bindings as she moaned nonsensical noises into the tape, shaking her head. The woman's reaction told Hannah she didn't want to do anything this man suggested. Hannah struggled against the grip on her arm as Cassidy stirred more.

"Hand her over, Ivan."

Pleasure crossed Grant's face, and the emptiness in Hannah's stomach churned up bile. Her hands cradled her middle. Her feet had a difficult time keeping up as Ivan forced her into Grant's waiting hands. His grip was no gentler than Ivan's. His other hand slid up the fabric of the skimpy dress Kenzie had forced her into she didn't know how many days ago. Was it yesterday or longer ago than that?

She tried to take a step back to get the material out of his hands. His exposed teeth had her stumbling. The only thing keeping her from falling to the floor was his viselike grip on her arm. He pulled her closer to his chest.

"Got anythin' on under here?" He tugged on the material of her dress. "Guess we'll find out."

A squeak escaped her lips as he dragged her across the warehouse floor. In one corner, metal chairs surrounded a folding table with cards scattered across the top. That must have been where the men were sitting.

Grant shoved her into a small bathroom and indicated a rack with track suits on it. "Put that on."

The woman sitting on the other cot was wearing similar clothes. When Hannah made no move to change, Grant stepped forward. The heat from his body raced over her exposed back. He tucked a finger under the strap of her dress and started to move it down over her shoulders. Terrified, she stepped forward, turning to face him.

"I can get it!" she snapped, her voice a hoarse rasp she didn't recognize as her own.

He spread his arms out in front of himself as if to say, "By all means." Taking a few steps away from him, she kept her back to him as she pulled the pants on under the dress.

"Ahh, c'mon, sweetheart, that makes it no fun."

The bile she feared losing all over the warehouse floor made another appearance. She needed to stay focused—pragmatic. Tugging the hoodie from the hanger, she knew she wouldn't be able to get it on without taking off the dress. Tugging the dress over her head, she felt more exposed than ever in just her bra and the velvet pants. The bruises on her arms ached as she forced them through the sleeves. With a decisive zip, she turned back to find

Grant looming over her. She hadn't heard him come any closer while she was changing. The fact that he could move that swiftly and quietly had more anxiety settling in her belly.

He leaned in, tucking a strand of hair behind her ear. Whenever she'd seen that same gesture in a movie, she'd thought it was so sweet—romantic, even. This touch was nothing of the sort.

"Dress was better," he said as if he was mentally redressing her.

He escorted her back out the door to find Ivan standing there, holding Cassidy, waiting for the restroom. Her large chocolate eyes were red and darting around. Her beautiful black hair was filled with hay wedged into the curls.

"Cassidy," she cried as she was propelled forward, back to the cots. They reminded her of the ones she'd seen when watching military movies with her father.

"Han," Cassidy croaked as tears spilled down her cheeks.

Hannah wanted to hold her or hug her, but the grip on her arm was forcing her away from her best friend. Cassidy was emotional, and Hannah was worried about her being alone with that man.

The older man in glasses was at the truck that must have brought them here. An old horse trailer was hooked to it, and the hay bales lying around the warehouse floor would explain the hay she'd seen in her and Cassidy's hair.

Hannah had no sooner hit the unforgiving seat of her cot when Cassidy screamed from the bathroom. Both she and the other woman began to struggle as Kenzie started to wriggle. The woman bound to the cot pulled against her bindings, and the skin around her wrists was bright red.

"Sit the fuck down," Grant barked. "Or ya'll be bound like her."

With one last shove from Grant, she fell down to sit on the edge of her cot. Glaring up at him, she knew her best option was to not end up tied to it. So rather than do anything more, she sat and waited—for far longer than she thought it should take for someone to get changed. After all, it had only taken her a moment.

She feared what might be happening to Cassidy, and her mind ran wild with the possibilities. Finally, the door of the bathroom swung open again. Cassidy emerged, head bowed, curls covering her face, wearing the same tracksuit. Hannah was about to stand when Grant grabbed her jaw in one of his large hands.

"Look at me," he hissed, his hollow eyes showing he had zero qualms with what they were doing. He even looked like he was enjoying himself. "If you so much as move ya ass one inch, ya gunna find yourself strapped too."

Pushing her face away from him, he made his way over to Kenzie then hauled her off to the bathroom next. While Cassidy was redeposited in her spot, Ivan spun her to sit facing the other woman and Hannah.

"Cass, are you all right?" Hannah whispered, leaning in close to get a better look at her friend. But her eyes were still trained on the floor. She wasn't blinking. "Cass?" she hissed.

Cassidy did little more than shake her head. Her eyes were wide as if processing everything. She was a smart girl, and Hannah knew she must know she needed to keep her wits about her. They couldn't afford for any of them to shut down.

"Cass, snap out of it," she said, feeling frustration welling in her eyes. She'd always hated that she was one of those people who cried when she was angry. Her sharp tone earned her a glare from the woman next to her. Hannah ignored it. Obviously, she had more sense than her if she didn't end up bound with her mouth taped shut.

"Sam, are you swapping out the trailers?" Ivan called from his chair at the card table.

Sam grunted something that sounded affirmative and continued what he was doing.

Ivan bolted out of his chair and went into a door to the left.

"Cass," Hannah said again, more softly.

Cassidy's large eyes met hers. They were filled with tears, and more streamed down her cheeks. The paths looked etched into her skin.

"Han, where's Jenny?"

Hannah had nearly forgotten about her. She'd only thought of Jenny briefly when she'd been taken to the restroom. Shame filled her middle in the places where the anxiety hadn't already taken up residence.

"I don't know," Hannah admitted, bowing her head.

The woman next to her shifted in her seat.

"Do you know?"

The woman nodded, sadness spilling over the edge of her eyes.

Cassidy reached out and removed the tape from the woman's lips, revealing red, irritated skin.

She grimaced. There was a large gash on the side of her head. It was only visible because of the way her head dipped.

Hannah couldn't help but worry about what she was going to say. She had a sinking feeling that she didn't want to hear what the woman would say, that once it was said, it could never be taken back. The truth couldn't be changed.

"I'm sorry. Your friend didn't make it." Another tear raced down the woman's cheek. "I tried to resuscitate her. Nothing worked." Her voice cracked with emotion as she explained all she'd tried to do for their friend.

Seeing someone she didn't know heartbroken over losing Jenny made Hannah's breath catch in her throat. It was as if a balloon was inflated in her windpipe, getting larger and larger each time she tried to speak. Each time she wanted to swallow, the balloon bloated just a little bit more. The feeling was amplified when she saw her own sadness reflected in Cassidy.

Cassidy's chin quivered as more tears spilled over. Hannah was torn between wanting to cry and staying strong. She wanted to prove to these men that they were not going to break her. And perhaps they wouldn't. Perhaps it would be the love she'd always had for these girls that was going to break her. She wasn't sure what fate was going to bring her way. This, she thought glancing around them, was never in her mind as a possibility for her.

"Who are you? Where did they take you from?" Cassidy's abrupt question brought Hannah back to the moment, to the stranger who had tried to save their friend. The woman had tried so hard to fight that it had resulted in her being restrained. Hannah felt guilty for the smug thoughts that had plagued her mind before. Always being quick to assume the worst of others was an issue.

"I was at a motel in New Mexico. I'm Maria," she whispered.

Cassidy nodded. "We were at a resort in Mexico." Cassidy was fidgeting with the sleeves of her sweatshirt, wiping away each tear before it could make it far down her cheeks. She always fidgeted when something was bothering her. For once, Hannah knew she didn't need to prompt Cassidy to pull the information out of her.

Hannah suddenly noticed how long Kenzie had been gone. It felt like they'd been taken a lifetime ago. She was beginning to question her internal clock and her ability to estimate time. Everything around her was moving far too slow yet not slow enough. Too much was happening, and she wanted everything to stop. Peering at the bathroom door, she listened. No sounds came from the direction of the bathroom. She wasn't sure if she should be relieved or not.

As if on cue, the door to the bathroom was flung open. Cassidy quickly retaped Maria's mouth. Rather than protest, she leaned forward to make it easier for Cassidy. It was strange the way something terrible could immediately bond people.

Hannah knew at once that Maria was going to be an ally in this deadly territory. Her heart broke at the thought, and she, too, shed tears for Jenny, who had wanted nothing more than to fit in with the other girls. Hannah wondered if this was the first moment she'd ever taken the time to think of why Jenny was always so enthusiastic about what Kenzie wanted to do. Was she ever actually excited to do those things, or was it just because she wanted to fit in?

"Cass, Han..." Kenzie's gaze darted from her friends to Maria. "Where—" Her voice cracked. "Where's Jenny?" Her face crumpled before either of them spoke up.

Hannah didn't know how to force the words out.

"Sit down," Grant snapped as he forced Kenzie back down. She was wearing the last track suit that had been on the rack. They had been expecting four girls. And that was what they'd gotten.

CHAPTER SEVEN
MARIA, JULY 3RD

With one arm still fastened to the underside of the old cot, she fed herself the sandwich Ivan had thrust upon her. She had been skeptical when taking her first bite, afraid of what might have been hidden between the slices of dry bread. It scratched at her throat as she swallowed. A drink would be nice, she thought as she watched the other girls choke down their sandwiches.

Sam bustled out from what Maria assumed was the office, where Frank seemed to stay hidden. In his arms were four bottled waters. She could have cried out with relief. With a small, sad smile, he extended a water to each of them. Kenzie, who had seemed to still be in shock, just sat there holding her sandwich and staring into space. Maria took the girl's water and placed it next to her. She was unblinking, taking an inordinately long time to chew each bite.

"Thank you," Cassidy whispered as she took her water from Sam. To Cassidy's credit, Maria hadn't even considered thanking the man.

Hannah all but scoffed at her manners. "They're all holding us here against our will, and you're thanking them for a damn water?"

"I suppose he could have left us to become dehydrated," Cassidy snapped.

Ivan and Grant looked up from their own lunch and game of cards. Their twin scowls did nothing more than increase the agitation in Maria's middle.

"We shouldn't argue amongst ourselves," Maria whispered. "We're all one another has. We have to work together to get out of this."

"You think we can?" This, from Kenzie, was a shock. She hadn't spoken since the news of Jenny had been discussed.

Maria couldn't bring herself to answer. It was probably the most difficult question she'd ever been asked. She washed down the bread and mystery meat with water, contemplating what she should say. Foregoing any words, she simply shrugged. They continued to eat in near silence.

Inspiration struck. "So," Maria began, leaning in closer to the others and lowering her voice. The lack of movement in one of her arms made it difficult, but she would suffer for this, for the chance of generating a plan that could save them all. "I think they're going to put us in that trailer." She hitched her chin toward the new trailer Sam had brought into the warehouse. Apparently, they didn't like to use the same one twice in a row.

The others nodded their understanding. "When they're getting ready to put us in there, we need to create a commotion, do something to get them flustered. Then maybe one of us will be able to run out of here, get help. I don't know how far from a city we are, but they wouldn't be able to send everyone to chase after one person."

"I don't understand. You think they'll open the door before we're loaded?" Hannah asked, her brows furrowing together.

"Well, no," Maria admitted. "But I did watch Sam when he shut the door. There is a key that needs to be inserted into the lock to move the door. The key was given to Grant." She could barely speak his name without a shiver running over her. The thought of his hands being anywhere near her had her heart picking up its pace. "I think they're going to drug us again." That was another thought she hated to have to consider. "The key is in Grant's front left pocket of his jacket. One of us might be able to grab it while they're sedating us. And judging from what I've seen of that asshole, I bet he'll want to be part of that."

They all looked to the man in question. He appeared to be having one of the best days of his life. "Who wants to do that?" Kenzie asked, her eyes still affixed to what Maria assumed was Grant's profile.

"I'll do it if it's convenient. Would anyone else be willing to try?" Maria felt guilty for even posing the question and asking one of the others to go along with her crazy plan. She grew more and more nervous as the others shared a look. None of them looked willing to take the chance. At least in her experience, these men weren't going to be easily fooled.

"I will," Hannah volunteered. "Do you know where we are?"

Relieved that it wasn't all going to lie on her shoulders, Maria sighed.

"No." Maria looked around the warehouse as if the window-less walls would be able to give her a hint as to where they were. "I was taken in New Mexico," she said again, wondering if the shock of everything made her forget.

"So, we're back in the US..." She trailed off, furrowing her brow. "I think I remember something," Hannah said, her face turning pale. "Oh my god." She whipped her hand to her mouth.

"Spit it out," Cassidy whispered, the urgency in her voice ringing out around them.

"Sorry," she said with chagrin. "I remember us coming across the border. Until now, I thought it was a really strange dream, but now, I think it actually happened. We were in a minivan. It had three rows of seats. I was in the middle row with Jenny. They rolled the windows down when we came across the border. The border patrolman was counting us. Laughing. He looked at the guy driving the van and said, 'Looks like a pretty lot.' I thought this was a weird thing to say. And then the officer held his hand out."

Dread filled Maria's belly. She knew what that meant. These men had this all planned out, and this likely wasn't their first time. That would explain their nonchalance. They'd been getting away with it.

"Then the man driving the truck slapped a stack of bills into the officer's extended palm. Then they shook hands and laughed. They actually laughed." Hannah's voice was losing its vigor as she spoke.

The thought that law officers were also involved heightened Maria's anxiety.

Now they had to wait for the men to do what they needed to execute their plan. And if miracles happened, then the women would escape.

CHAPTER EIGHT
AERON, JULY 2ND

"Finally," Aeron barked when Sam answered his phone.

"Sorry. It's been hectic today," Sam muttered.

Anything being hectic was not a good thing. Only a shit-storm would follow those words.

"Lay it on me."

After a long sigh, Sam dove straight to the issue. "One of those girls from the Mexico resort, she's dead. Ivan and I moved her body."

Aeron didn't have to ask where they had moved her body to.

"That's not all," Sam added.

A groan bordering on a growl escaped Aeron's lips. "Their, uh, their parents have been all over the news, asking for help finding them. They've offered some pretty hefty rewards."

Fuck. This is going to be an issue for a while. Missing person reports were one thing. Offering a reward was another. How could those guys in Mexico have fucked things up this royally?

"Let me think on this," Aeron said.

As he was about to disconnect his phone, Sam rushed to speak again. "Aeron, wait."

"What?" he barked, wondering what other hurricane of shit was going to be thrown his way.

"They took a woman from the motel. The clerk fucked up and let someone check in." Sam's words were rushed as if speaking them quickly would lessen the blow.

"So, we're looking at another missing persons report, potentially linked to the motel. How the hell does this happen?"

Sam gave him a quick explanation on how the clerk had not only let someone check in but also put her in a room directly next to the other girls.

What a fucking moron.

When Sam was done with his report, Aeron wanted to throw his phone across the room, the room he'd spent more time in than he wanted to think about. The one that was eventually going to lead him to a different life, he hoped. Tossing the phone onto the foot of the couch, he let out a frustrated groan. The thought of one of those women dying was an issue, for more reasons than the others knew.

After sitting for far longer than he should have, he got up off the couch and tromped out to the compact floor of what used to be a waiting room for a small family medical practice. He found two of the men setting up the equipment for them to ensure the girls were all hydrated. On one of the runs, a girl had collapsed, and it had been difficult to do anything with her because she was so dehydrated. Aeron swore that would never happen again. More fucking work when someone wasn't physically able to perform as she was supposed to.

Aeron wondered if anyone had informed Patrick of the issue. Issue? You ass, it's death, Aeron corrected himself. Her death wasn't an issue. It was unfortunate and terrible.

CHAPTER NINE
HANNAH, JULY 2ND

Sam was removing the last of the IV stands. Hannah assumed whatever they had pumped into each of the women was something to keep them hydrated, because she didn't feel any different. Grant strutted around, getting things loaded into the truck, and she couldn't help but watch Sam out of the corner of her eye. He was carefully measuring out syringes. She'd never particularly liked needles, but this brought it to an all-new level.

After their lunch, Maria, who she was beginning to like for her thoughtfulness, had both hands restrained. She should have asked what Maria had done to get tied down. She must be more persistent and braver than Hannah thought herself capable of. Hannah wanted to make a difference, especially now. They needed to work together to create a distraction so someone would be able to get the key from Grant.

The big oaf walked around like he owned the place and had life by the balls. She hated the feeling she got from him. Something in those cold eyes told her that if he had an opportunity to take advantage of any of them, he would certainly take it. Although she didn't think he'd tried anything when they were all forced to change, Cassidy hadn't said anything about what had made her scream when she was changing.

"Cass?" After waiting until she looked up, she continued. "Why did you scream earlier? When you were getting changed."

A shudder ran over Cassidy's thin arms, and goose bumps covered her dark skin where her sleeves were pushed up.

Sickness worked its way up Hannah's throat. She probably shouldn't have asked.

"Ivan tried to help me get undressed," she said, tears welling in her eyes. "I tried to back away from him and tripped over my own feet. I screamed when I fell. He just laughed at me, didn't help me up. Just stood over me, laughing."

Hannah didn't know why, but there was something in the way she said it. Her belly roiled with anger—no it was something more. Something darker.

"Then when I did stand back up, he all but ripped my dress off me. I was too stunned to do anything. How stupid is that?" Her breath was coming in short gasps.

Hannah launched herself toward her friend. Wrapping her arms around her neck, she pulled her close. Cassidy's warm tears slid down Hannah's neck.

"You didn't do anything wrong. Freezing is a natural reaction," Hannah cooed as she held Cassidy close.

"Get back in ya fuckin' seat!" Grant barked as he made his way over to them.

Hannah's eyes grew large. She wondered if she should take this as her moment to attempt to get the key. She turned to consult Maria, who gave an almost imperceptible shake of her head. Feeling herself deflate, she gave Cassidy one last squeeze before dropping back down on her cot, glaring up at Grant.

"Stay in ya damn seat," Grant said, leaning in close. His warm breath sent a disgusted shiver down Hannah's back. He pulled a zip tie from his back pocket.

Hannah's eyes were the size of grapefruits. How were either she or Maria going to get the key if they were both tied down?

Hannah shook her head. "I won't get up again, please," she said, trying to soften her expression. She tried to make herself look as innocent and pleading as possible.

"This ain' my first rodeo." Grant laughed, and his breath smelled of cigarettes and made her want to curl her upper lip and lean away from him. Yanking her arms down, he strapped her wrists together. When she tried to pull away from him, he leaned in closer to her, whispering in her ear, "Ya get me hard when ya struggle."

After strapping her hands to the underside of her cot, he stood to put the proof of his erection in her face. She couldn't lean back. Turning her head away to stare at the wall, her eyes welling with tears, was her only option. She'd messed up and let her emotions get the best of her. His heavy footsteps backing away from her gave her leave to relax for a moment.

"Ya need a shoulder to cry on?" Grant asked, looming over Cassidy. The closer he leaned in, the more Hannah could see Maria struggling against the bindings around her wrists. The muffled sounds coming from her were angry, while her violent movements caused blood to trickle from her wrists. Hannah was stunned to see how hard she was struggling for someone she'd just met.

Cassidy leaned away from him, shaking her head. Barely turning around, Grant slapped Maria across the face. The impact echoed around the small warehouse. Maria pointed an angry glare at Grant. Hannah assumed that if she weren't already tied down, Maria would have been trying to claw his eyes out.

"Damn it, Grant, get your ass over here and get shit done," Frank said as he made his way to the trailer. "We need them to look decent, not like they've been brawling."

Hannah hated to think of them being stuffed into another trailer. Although she didn't remember anything about the trek here, she wasn't looking forward to being moved again. Kenzie, who always had something to say, had been silent most of the afternoon. It was strange to see someone be reduced to such a depressive state, especially when it was someone who was always ready to come up with a quip like it was the most natural thing in the world. Following her gaze, Hannah figured she was focused on her feet.

Maria was still seething, and a red patch was revealing itself where Grant's hand had caught her. She seemed oblivious to the state of both her wrists and her face.

"Maria, you're bleeding," Hannah said, leaning over to look as closely as she could at the other woman's hands. Furrowing her brows, she shifted her eyes to where Hannah's rested.

Maria's brows shot up. As Maria took in a deep breath, her chest rose, and her eyes closed. She was holding herself together remarkably well.

"I'm sorry," Cassidy whispered, looking between them.

Hannah and Maria shook their heads at her in unison.

"We're in this together," Hannah told her. "No matter the situation, I will do anything to fight for all of us." Hannah could feel a lump forming in her throat. She wondered if her fighting would result in rape or some other form of abuse.

Somehow, Frank had made his way over to them without Hannah noticing. His sudden appearance caused her to jump, sending a tidal wave of pain from her wrists up her arms and into her core. *How had Maria fought so hard when this small movement caused me so much pain?*

"You," he said, forcing Maria into his shadow.

She sat tall, or as tall as she could in her bindings, and stared back at him. Hannah was in awe of her—she needed to act more like her.

"You're going to be first since you don't fucking listen," Frank announced, jamming a needle into her arm. Hannah didn't notice the syringe in his hand, and clearly, neither had Maria. Her posture relaxed slowly as the drug made its way through her small, feisty body. It was then Hannah realized it was truly all on her. Kenzie and Cassidy would likely panic in the moment.

Maria's bindings were cut as Frank lifted her into his arms. Hannah didn't miss the way his hands felt up her body. It was disgusting how he had no qualms with taking advantage of an unconscious woman—likely none of these men did. It was apparently time to go. The other three men approached each of them. Grant was the one to approach Cassidy, and the hair on the back of Hannah's neck stood at attention. The fear filling Cassidy's eyes broke her. Sam was in front of Kenzie, which left Ivan coming for her. Great.

Ivan crouched to cut the ties from under the cot before giving her the sedative. Her wrists were still tied together, but this would be her only moment. She shot to her feet, and the top of her head caught Ivan in the nose. She heard a stomach-flipping crunch. Oh, gosh, did I break his nose?

"Fuck," Ivan shouted.

Trying to focus only on the key Grant had, she rushed at him while he was bent over Cassidy. At the sound of Ivan's shout, he turned his head to see her coming. Her heart was pounding in her ears. She swore she could hear the blood moving with each pulse, each beat of her heart. Hands bound together, she knew getting the key was going to be difficult, but she had to try. As her hands reached for his pocket, Ivan's body pressed against her back. His arms wrapped around her front, pulling her to his chest. She could feel something hot running down her neck, and she knew it must be blood. The thought of someone else's blood running over her body sent panic rushing into her chest, igniting her fight or flight. She was thankful it was flight that coursed through her veins, mingling with the blood flowing to every extremity. Kicking her feet wildly, she tried to catch either Grant or Ivan. At this moment, she didn't care which of them she hit. She hoped she distracted them both enough that one of the other girls would go for the key in Grant's pocket.

As she fought, both the others sat watching her. She hated the way they didn't move to help. They just watched, eyes wide. They all needed to fight. What are they doing? She could feel resentment building inside her.

"Let me go!" she shouted, trying to wriggle her arms out of Ivan's grip as Grant stepped out of the reach of her legs.

Something sharp was pressed into her arm, and she turned to see Sam looking at her sadly from behind his glasses. Before she could make a coherent thought or move, her eyes drifted closed as her body relaxed against Ivan's without her permission.

CHAPTER TEN
MARIA, JULY 3RD

Maria was too tired to even attempt opening her eyes as the telltale squeak of metal on metal let her know the door to the trailer was being opened. Rustling told her they were again removing hay bales. Her throat was dry, and swallowing was painful. The trailer shook as the men climbed in. She'd slept for the entire ride this time. Unsure if she should be happy or not, she chanced a look around the trailer. It was surprisingly bright. She had assumed it would be dark just as it had been the morning before.

She could see outside here. The trailer was outside. Rolling onto her side, she wished she had the energy to run. Coming off whatever this drug was slowed her brain function along with her movements. It hadn't been nearly this bad the day before.

Grant entered the trailer, and she let her eyes shut again. Not seeing his pompous face would be best. Pretending to be a ragdoll was not necessary today. She couldn't have lifted her head if she'd wanted to. It was as if her neck no longer had the strength for the simple task of looking around a room. She was lifted into the arms of a man she wished she'd never met. Watching the world upside down was going to make her sick.

Why can't I do anything? I should be running away. Why won't my body cooperate?

She ventured another glance when Grant's steps slowed and the chill of air conditioning swept across her face.

"Where ya want 'em?" Grant asked in his hillbilly way.

A man in a medical coat stood before her. "I'm not sure. Do they need their exams first?"

Footsteps slapped across the tiles. Grant turned toward the sound, and the spinning had Maria wondering if she was going to lose the abysmal contents of her stomach. Snapping her eyes shut, she focused on the sounds. The steps stopped, and a low growl filled the space.

"Maria? What the hell are you doing?" When he spoke her name, a chill surged down her spine. She recognized the voice immediately, but she couldn't force her eyes open. Hiding from the truth was better than reality, she assured herself. Especially now. Shaking her head, she felt a headache fill her jostled brain. Her entire body ached. How did I go from needing a break at work to being kidnapped? I would take Dean and his misogyny over this.

Maria forced open her puffy eyes, lifting her head to see the man standing in front of her. She needed to face her reality no matter the consequences. No matter the heartbreak, she would endure. When her eyes connected with his, the name was an anguished whisper on the breath knocked out of her. "Aeron?" An ache in her chest threatened to extinguish all the hope she had left.

Jolted out of her hazy awakening by recognition, she pushed herself from Grant's arms and clumsily landed on her feet. Cringing from the pain shooting through her limbs, she braced herself on the arm of a man she once would have trusted with her soul. The intense blue eyes she had known so well were roving all over her body.

She knew she must look a mess after two nights in hay-filled trailers, no access to a shower, and limited access to a bathroom.

"Who decided to bring her here?" Aeron's shout terrified her, but she refused to let go of the one thing she recognized. She had never seen him angry, not like this. The muscles in his arm were tense as he looked between Grant and Sam.

"She was at the motel," Grant replied, obviously assuming this would be sufficient. She was astounded to see her wrists weren't bound together anymore.

Aeron's eyes swung to Grant over her shoulder. The rage emanating from Aeron's face and stance was enough to halt any further excuses. "You." Aeron looked pointedly to Grant, who Maria would imagine was reflecting the irritation in Aeron's piercing gaze. "You were supposed to pick up the four girls from the Mexican resort. How did you get the wrong fucking person?"

"We figured one extra would be good. Especially now, since one of the girls from Mexico died," Grant replied.

Maria's legs shook under the casual way he mentioned Jenny's death.

"I think Patrick would agree."

At the mention of Patrick's name, Maria's knees went weak. She was going to collapse. This can't be happening. How could he be involved? This is a mistake. A different Patrick. Her breathing came in short, rapid spurts. Too much was coming at her all at once.

She looked up at Aeron with pleading eyes. Ignoring her stare, he bore down on the other man. "Well, he might, but I think he would be happier if the woman you grabbed wasn't his fucking sister!"

The exclamation shattered her. Two direct hits in quick succession. She couldn't stand. She wanted to scream at him and tell him he was wrong, but how could she? She only saw her brother on the obligatory holidays. When she did, he was reserved and hostile. Something had happened between him and their parents, and neither ever spoke of the conflict. Not that he was ever one to turn to her to talk about anything, never mind a disagreement he had with their parents.

Maria felt every pair of eyes on her, and the man in the white medical coat shifted his weight from one foot to the other. How could my brother and his best friend have concocted this plan?

This is not real. She looked around herself. Three men surrounded her. One, she'd always thought would be there for her. During her youth, he'd always stood up for her. He was a better older brother than the man she shared genetics with. But instead of having an ally, she was being watched by three strangers. Three disgusting criminals. More were probably lurking in the building.

The other three girls were still in the trailer, being watched by Sam. Over Aeron's broad shoulder, she could tell this was a drastic change from the warehouse. She took in the room. The frosted-glass windows had grates. She was frozen to the spot.

A shift in the air met her when Grant left the room. He returned moments later with Kenzie. She shifted in his hands, and they walked past. Maria felt that familiar lump in her throat. This time, it was because she feared there was little she would be able to do. Calling Patrick had been the first thing she was going to do, but now, she knew that wasn't an option. She tried to look around, to stanch the tears trying to escape. Her vision was blurring. She couldn't see past the sadness clouding her. Everything was crumbling at her feet.

My brother can't be responsible for someone's death. This must have been some kind of mistake.

Aeron grabbed her by the upper arm and pulled her along behind him. The pain in her limbs was forgotten amid the chaos of being recognized. A thick haze had filled her body the moment she'd recognized Aeron's voice. But the reality of her body's condition was brought back full force as she began walking again. The muscles throughout her ached, even the ones she hadn't realized she'd used the day before. Pain radiated from her head to her feet and extended to her aching hands. In his presence, all the pain from her past, even beyond the last two days, swarmed her body, stinging like relentless hornets.

"Aeron, what's going on?" she asked weakly, the lump in her throat increasing. It was difficult to breathe let alone speak.

Ignoring her, he shoved her into a small office. "Sit down," he growled. "And if you try to come out this door"—he tilted his head toward the door she'd just been forced through—"there will be two men on the other side. Now, I'll be back in a moment." He slammed the door in her face.

She didn't know how to take control of a situation in which she was so severely outnumbered. Escape was her only hope. Then she would need to find a way to lead the police back to these men —and Aeron. Her heart sputtered at the thought of both Aeron and her brother in police custody.

Pivoting slowly, Maria took inventory of everything in the office. Three chairs sat around a small table with a sofa to the left of the table. One four-drawer filing cabinet sat in the corner. Nothing was on the table. No papers, pencils, pens, or notes. No phone. What kind of office is this?

She found a phone jack on the wall behind the table, next to the filing cabinet. Maria limped to the cabinet then shakily tried to open each of the drawers in turn. Each time she curled her fingers around the handles, she was reminded of the trauma she and the others had endured and the lacerations on her wrists. Locked. Frustrated, she shook the last drawer in an attempt to get it open. She groaned when it didn't budge any farther than the rest.

There was a small set of wooden cabinets on the opposite wall. She hastened over to check their contents. Before she could get to the first cupboard handle, the office door swung open, slamming off the wall on the opposite side.

"Making yourself right at home, I see," Aeron said snidely, closing the door behind himself. "Sit," he demanded, indicating a chair on the other side of the table and taking the seat by the filing cabinet.

"Not until you or someone else tells me what is going on here," she said with as much force as she could muster. She was in shock, still unable to believe this could be real. She needed to find a way to contact her brother. She didn't believe he knew what was happening to those girls—she didn't want to believe. But the other men talked of him as if this were all his doing.

He propped his right ankle on his left knee like he had all the time in the world to wait for her to concede. All these men were infuriating. She was afraid of what he would tell her. Swallowing hard, she weighed her options—do as he asked or be difficult. Screw him. Turning her back to him, she opened the cabinet door and found paper cups and lids. Pushing them aside, she looked behind them. Nothing.

"Find what you're looking for?" She spun back around to face him.

A smirk spread across his face. It made her want to slap him, to flip the table between them. There was a time she'd thought of him as even more than a friend. *Well, I still would if I was seeing him under different circumstances.* The realization covered her face in a blush, while sickness roiled in her stomach. The conflicting emotions were enough to exhaust her further. She didn't have the energy for all of this. It had now been days since she'd gotten a proper and full night's sleep.

His black hair was just as dark as it ever was, longer on the top while shorter on the sides. That, at least, hadn't changed, and it still worked for him. His strong jaw was stubborn and unrelenting, covered in a thick, short beard. Out in the other room, she couldn't help but notice the well-defined muscles of his arms as she clung to him for support. Although his legs looked relaxed in his jeans, she knew they were powerful. If he needed to assert himself against someone, it would be no contest.

Giving him one more irritated glance, she limped to the door.

"I wouldn't go back out there if I were you."

"And why is that?" she demanded, whirling around irritably.

"The others want to take you to one of the exam rooms like the other women to keep you from..." He indicated her bloody wrists and hands. What he couldn't see were her bruised knees and arms. His glancing over her body didn't give him the full picture of what she'd been through. "I think otherwise."

She let her hand drop from the knob. "What is going on here, Aeron? What do you guys think you're doing with all these girls?" Her voice rose with anger and fear as she advanced on him. He didn't seem to care about her anger or her closeness.

"Delivering them."

His simple statement sent a shiver up her spine as a boulder settled into her stomach. "To who? What the hell are you doing? One of those girls died! You heard that, right?" Maria's voice cracked as she held her tears at bay.

His impassive expression faltered for a moment, but he recovered quickly, which made her want to strangle him. The urge to lash out for Jenny was hard to suppress. How could he not care about another person's life? She had seen him with other people, and he was always a bit pompous, but he had never struck her as someone who would so easily turn a blind eye to someone who was injured or dead.

"I gave her CPR for who knows how long, trying to save her." Her voice broke a little more with each word. She could see herself giving the compressions, leaning over the poor girl's body, willing her to live. The small features of her face and her long, flowing hair lay in the hay. It would be the image of Maria's nightmares for the rest of her life, however long that might be. "What about her family? Will they ever know what happened to her?"

She watched, waiting for him to answer just one of her questions. She was met with nothing but a cool stare, and she wasn't sure how she should take the silence. "Why aren't you answering me?"

Her voice was becoming weaker with emotion. The boulder in her stomach was dragging her down, making her wish she could curl up on the floor, to hold herself together, because surely, this boulder was about to explode. She didn't want to cry anymore.

"There is nothing I can do for her now," he said quietly, rising from the chair and striding to the door. "Sit down."

Heeding his words, she lowered herself slowly into the chair.

"Stay here," he said, barely meeting her gaze.

"Aeron, wait," she begged.

He turned to meet her eyes.

"Please don't make me go back in that trailer." She would plead with everything she had. She couldn't be in there again. The smell of the wet hay. Knowing that another girl had died in one of the trailers with her. Reliving those moments in the trailer was next on her list of things she never wanted.

"Do you have any idea what you are asking of me? What this could do to me and everyone else?" he asked, fury radiating off of him.

She thought about shaking her head, but she knew he was asking rhetorically. Her answer would likely just piss him off even more. So instead, she waited.

With a sharp nod, he started toward the door then turned back to her. He leaned close over her. Looking up into his eyes, she was startled when he strapped both of her wrists to the arms of the chair. Without another word, he exited.

Maria could see three other men milling about. She couldn't see the girls and wasn't sure how she felt about that. Aeron had mentioned an exam room. She felt guilty for her moment of weakness, begging to receive special treatment. The others didn't know she knew Aeron. They also didn't know it was apparently her own family who had created this ring of deceit, tragedy, and heinous activity. She soon found there weren't adequate words to describe what they were doing. She only hoped she could stop it.

She struggled against her bindings. The ties dug into her raw flesh as she struggled. She wanted to be able to see and hear what was going on. Aeron and two of the others were in a closed circle, whispering. She leaned toward the open door in the hopes of hearing what they might be talking about.

Sam nodded and began speaking. Wishing she could read lips, she focused on the movements of his mouth. Aeron listened intently, bowing his head slightly as he closed his eyes. She tensed, gripping the arm of the chair. He did care. She could see it in the way his brows pulled together. It was a look she'd seen whenever he heard about Patrick treating her poorly.

The three of them split up.

Aeron's eyes found hers. She thought she could see an apology there, but as soon as the sadness appeared, it vanished. If she hadn't known him so well, she might have missed it. She silently berated herself for thinking she knew him at all. Maybe she used to. But maybe, even then, she hadn't known him at all. There was definitely something in his eyes. The way he looked at her conveyed something—she knew she was foolish to hope it meant what she thought it did.

Aeron stalked back to the office but only came close enough to soundly slam the door in her face. It was impossible to make out any words being said on the other side. For a while, she didn't hear anything. She tried again to escape the ties. Each movement only burrowed the ties deeper into the skin below. The burning fueled her anger and determination.

CHAPTER ELEVEN
AERON, JULY 3RD

Shaking, Aeron made his way back to the other men, fury boiling in every limb. He wanted to beat Grant then drive to the motel and find the new guy.

It had been Grant who had insisted on taking Maria from the motel. He knew Grant couldn't let her walk away after nearly being kidnapped, but that still didn't stop the rage from welling inside him. He didn't trust Grant as far as he could throw him. If he'd been asked to guess who the woman taken from the motel was, Maria wouldn't have been included in his first ten guesses.

He needed to call Patrick. One run had never gone this far awry. One woman was dead, one wasn't supposed to be on the trailer, and of course, that woman was one he'd been fantasizing about for far too long. She'd been out of reach and off limits for longer than he wanted to think about. Fuck.

With a long sigh, he unlocked his phone to call Patrick.

"Aeron, got a minute?" Sam stood to the side of the waiting room, looking at the door to the hall.

"Sure," Aeron muttered, grateful for the momentary reprieve. He was more nervous about what Patrick would likely say than he wanted to admit.

Following Sam out of the building, he looked one last time at the office door, where the woman he both wanted and needed was within. But now, will she ever be able to look past this? Will she ever understand?

Sam broke into his thoughts. "That girl," he said, shifting his gaze to the trailer he and Grant had driven to the old physician's office. Although they were outside, there was little chance that anyone would see them. They were at the end of a mostly deserted industrial park. Aeron wasn't sure if he was talking about Maria or the girl who'd died.

"Gotta be a bit more specific."

"The one that died. She was taken from that resort in Mexico. I've been seeing her photo and three others all over the news." They kept a small television in the breakroom at each of their stops because it came in handy to know about reports of the missing girls.

Aeron stared at a spot between the cedar shakes of the building. As he listened, the furrow between his brows deepened. "You told me this yesterday," Aeron snapped.

Sam shrugged. "She is one of the girls whose parents are very wealthy and are ready to do anything they can to get their daughter back."

The direness of the situation pressed in on him from all sides. If he were claustrophobic, he would likely be crumpled on the ground, gasping for breath. "What have they said?"

"Not really sure. I just seen them on TV last night begging whoever took their daughters to bring them back. They're offering a hefty reward for their safe return."

"Fuck," Aeron muttered, placing his hands on his hips, letting his head drop between his shoulders. "Any more good news?"

Sam almost flinched at the question. "Just that we need to hurry this along. The sooner this run is done, the better."

Aeron picked up on the deeper meaning of his words. He rubbed the back of his neck, trying to alleviate the stress that was settling in. Nodding, he clapped the older man on the shoulder. He was far smaller than Aeron but was more muscular than most of the other men knew. He was the only person Aeron had hired himself. That would remain the case—he had few people he would trust his life to.

The building ahead was filled with drugged women and men he couldn't trust. What a life he was living. Now the phone call to Patrick was all the more important. People could be bought, but they had to be the highest bidder. He doubted they would be paying more than these parents would be, and that could ruin everything. These men could flip at a moment's notice.

Aeron pressed the call button. His blood chilled as he heard the steady ringing. He wished to get this over with. Once. Twice. Like most times, Patrick waited until the third ring.

"Aeron?" He sounded surprised. Aeron did his best to call only when absolutely necessary. This was more than necessary.

"Patrick, we have a situation." Foregoing any pleasantries, he dove in. "The four girls that were taken in Mexico have been all over national news. Parents are begging for their daughters back, offering high rewards for their safe return." Aeron rubbed the back of his neck as he spoke.

Patrick seemed amused as he spoke. "How much they offering?"

"I don't know exactly. Sam told me about the news reports."

"Too bad. If we can't make money on them one way, maybe we could on another." Patrick's sinister laugh sent ice running through Aeron's veins.

"This isn't a damn joke, Patrick. Those guys know they're supposed to take women who are on their own, not fucking groups of college girls." Taking a deep breath, Aeron prepared himself for the toughest part. "One of those girls is dead."

He let the weight of his declaration hang in the air around them.

"Dispose of her. What do you want me to do about it?" Patrick's heartless response had Aeron's temper rising.

"Her body was taken care of at the Eagle Warehouse, but you need to talk to your guy at the motel. He let someone check in to the hotel, and now, we have a girl here who shouldn't be."

Patrick scoffed as if the answer to the issue were obvious. "This is my operation, Aeron. Don't try to tell me how to run it. The new girl can take the dead girl's place." Patrick's voice reverberated through Aeron's head. It was laced with anger, as if Aeron were too stupid to consider the easy answer. "Plus, I told them to take the group," he growled. Questioning his decisions always put Patrick on the edge of rage.

"The other girl is Maria," Aeron said, almost in a whisper.

Patrick was quiet for a while. Hopefully, he was taking this issue seriously now. When minutes passed with no response, Aeron checked the screen of his cell phone to make certain the call hadn't been lost. The timer on his phone told him the call had been going for three minutes and continued ticking on.

"Patrick? You still there?"

Finally, he heard something on the other end of the call. Patrick's breathing was ragged. Maybe he was taking this seriously now. His little sister was now in the crossfire of his plan. Aeron knew this would change everything. But as he listened to his oldest friend's breathing, he realized he was not distraught or angry. He was laughing.

Patrick stopped laughing long enough to say, "Drug that little bitch too."

The call ended, and Aeron stared at the screen of his phone. He needed to make a decision. Now.

CHAPTER TWELVE
HANNAH, JULY 3RD

When she woke on what appeared to be an examination table, hope welled in her. An IV stand, much like the one from the night before, stood next to her head, but this room was different. The line in the IV was connected to her arm. Trying to sit up, she found her arms and legs were bound. Realization slapped her in the face. She was not in a hospital, and she was not being treated by a doctor. Her building optimism was crushed under the weight of what her life had become. This was made even worse when the door swung open and Grant entered along with another man. The new man wore a white lab coat.

"Ready for your exam?"

"My what?" she asked, her question escaping as a desperate plea.

Grant leered down at her.

Feeling vulnerable and shivering, she looked to the doctor.

The man shrugged, unzipping the front of the velour track suit she'd been forced into the day before. The cool air met her skin, prickling the edge of her sanity with anxiety. She was exposed—

granted, she still had on her bra—but she hated the feeling of someone looking at her like this.

The new man took a stethoscope from around his neck, and she tried to wriggle away from him. "Get away from me." She shifted as far away as she could with her right arm and leg strapped to the legs of the exam table. With her arms extended over her head, there was little she could do.

"The more you fight, the longer this is going to take," the man said, taking on a bored demeanor. "I need to check your vitals and do a pelvic exam."

Shame and fear washed over her. She knew her face must portray her emotions because she saw the way Grant shifted closer. The sick way he enjoyed her terror created a hollowness in her chest, as if it was going to cave in on itself. Instead, the cave housed all the fears she'd been trying to ignore. All the what-ifs multiplied to fill the space.

"I want him out, then," she said, turning to Grant.

The man looked down at her then up at Grant. "She is strapped down," the supposed doctor told Grant. "She's not going to get far."

Hannah knew better than to feel any sort of relief until Grant was actually out of the room. Grant's angry glare pierced the man.

"I'll be right outside the door. If ya need help, I'll be back." He focused his gaze on Hannah before backing out of the room. Taking a few calming breaths, she met the other man's deep-green eyes. There was almost a kindness buried in there.

"I am Dr. Bryne. I strictly want to do the exam. I am not here for anything else," he assured her.

It was probably foolish, but she allowed her body to relax into the table beneath her. The knowledge that Grant was out of the room did more for her than any kind of reward. He hadn't fought nearly as hard as she'd expected him to.

Dr. Bryne went about his work. Only silence and the sounds of the doctor moving about the room filled the air around her. It was difficult for her to stay still and cooperate. She wished she knew what was happening with the other girls. Taking a steadying breath, she tried to empty her mind, to try to focus on anything but the speculum being inserted, the discomfort. It was her least favorite part of a physical or annual exam. Not that she had a favorite part, but if she did, this certainly wasn't it. Still, his silence was better than the conversations her gynecologist always tried to have while down there.

When he stepped away from her and placed all his tools on the cart next to him, she let out a breath of relief.

"All right, I am going to pull your panties and pants back up." He stepped forward again and did just as he said.

It was disgusting, and she wanted to cry, but he'd done only as he said. There was nothing to any of his exam that caused her to step any further over the edge of horror.

The doctor checked the bag of clear liquid hanging at her head.

"What is that?"

"Just saline to keep you hydrated," he said as if it should have been obvious. "Done in here," Dr. Bryne called out.

The door swung open, and Grant's hard profile filled the doorway. "I'll bring ya to the next one." He strode over to Hannah's side and produced a knife from a sheath on his hip. The blade was ominous, and renewed fear rushed over her. With each tie he cut, she worried he was going to cut her, too, even if just to prove he could.

"Ya gunna behave today?" Grant asked, a glint of joy sparking behind his loveless eyes. It was almost as if he liked the women to be subdued but also enjoyed the fight they put up. Either reaction was fun for him.

Hannah nodded, not wanting to see what else he would be willing to do with the blade in hand.

Grant took hold of her bicep, pulled her off the table, then pushed her farther down a dark hall. He shoved Hannah into a dark room, and she stumbled as she made her way over the threshold. Once the door was locked, she fell to her hands and knees in the pitch black. She felt around the floor, crawling as she went.

"Han?" a small voice asked.

"Kenzie?" She crawled in the direction of the voice. "Are you all right?" she asked when she reached her and felt the other girl's leg. Embracing one another, they sat for a moment. "Is Cassidy in here too?"

"No, it was just me for a long time." Kenzie's voice broke. "What are we going to do? They did an exam on me. Like a pap and shit. Grant stood over the doctor the entire time. I hated it." Her voice broke as she walked Hannah through what had happened. Her emotions were enough to make anyone ill. It was as if they were on a roller coaster, being jostled and moved out of place as her body went through the loops and sharp curves.

"I don't know," Hannah admitted. She hated to say it, but at some point, she had to acknowledge that her fighting was doing nothing for any of them.

"I still can't believe Jenny's gone," Kenzie whispered into Hannah's hair.

Hannah wished she could see Kenzie's face. She hated herself for it, but deep down, she wanted to place the blame for this entire situation on Kenzie. It had been her harebrained idea to go down to that bar. Kenzie and her lust for a random man.

"I know you probably blame me," Kenzie said, her voice cracking. "I blame me."

For some reason, Kenzie's admission fueled the self-loathing running through Hannah's veins. There was no way this could all be pinned on Kenzie, and she felt terrible for even thinking it.

"Kenzie, you couldn't have known this would happen. We can't play the blame game. We need to hold each other together, work together." She needed to get away from the blaming. The judging. In that moment, she realized that was what she'd always done. That was likely the real reason she'd never been able to branch out from her childhood group of friends—she was too quick to judge others. She'd always judged Jenny for being Kenzie's cheerleader, while she did nothing but follow along too. She'd even judged Cassidy for always choosing her novels over other activities. She judged the way the other girls interacted with one another. In the darkness, there was endless time for self-reflection.

Hearing footsteps outside the door, Hannah crawled back to where she thought the door would be. Then someone else was propelled into the room.

"Cass?" Hannah and Kenzie chorused.

"Yeah," she rasped as Hannah felt for her in the darkness. The little light that had been momentarily let in made the room feel all the darker. "Guys, she's his sister," Cassidy whispered.

"Who is whose sister?" Hannah was beyond lost. Lost in the dark, in Cassidy's statement, in her own mind. In her own reality.

"Maria," she wailed. "Her brother runs this operation."

Hannah's mind raced as she wondered how that was possible. "I don't understand. Is she working with them?" Hannah rubbed her forehead as she tried to force understanding through her temples, as if her fingertips could push the information past the confusion.

"Do you think she was pretending to want to help us?" Cassidy gave voice to the fear and question that Hannah was struggling with.

"I don't know," Hannah said then hesitated before continuing. "Why would she be tied up and drugged if they knew her brother runs this? What kind of brother would do that?" Hannah was an only child, but Jenny had an older brother, and the thought of Jenny's brother sent a dagger into her heart. He was going to be devastated. He'd always been there for Jenny, helping her in any way she needed. Many times, he'd been the one to take the girls to and from different activities.

"I didn't see her in the front room," Cassidy said as Kenzie moved along the floor to join them. "And she's not in here with us."

As all three huddled together, Hannah couldn't keep her tears at bay. Hannah found herself shaking in anger. "I trusted her. I immediately thought she was one of us. That she would do anything like we would." Knowing Maria was not with them made her fear what kind of scheme this really was. What if everything she did and said yesterday was fake?

"How do you know it's her brother doing this?" Kenzie asked.

"Grant was telling the doctor while I was in the exam room. The doctor asked Grant if this was Patrick's way of checking on things."

Great, another man to worry about. This was another figure who could, and likely would, do everything in his power to keep her and her friends trapped in this.

The door to their small room swung open, and two imposing figures filled the doorway.

Chapter Thirteen
Maria, July 3rd

Maria had been so focused on listening to every little noise, she was startled when she heard a loud clattering from outside the door. She was expecting to hear something quiet and muffled, but what met her ears was almost as loud as a gunshot. Then she heard raised voices, but they were muffled enough to prevent her from distinguishing one word from the next.

She wondered if they were fighting about Jenny. There had definitely been something in Aeron's eyes. Maria thought of all the people who would miss the young woman, and fresh tears spilled from her eyes. Picturing all the people she loved and missed, Maria wondered if she would ever see them again. Knowing she would never hold them again burned a hole in her soul. Her parents' and Kameron's faces flashed before her eyes. The last thing she'd done was ignore them. Her desperation for a few hours of solace could have cost her everything.

She had told her parents she was going to stay at Patrick's motel, so maybe they would call in a missing person report. If her parents told them that was the last place she was going to go, then they might find her car and cell phone. But that was just a shot in the dark. With her ignoring everyone, would they actually call it in? They might wait days before reporting it since she'd made it known she wanted silence.

She was supposed to be on her trip too. She ticked off the days by tapping her fingers on the arm of the chair, thinking of what day it must be. Her processing was slowed, and she could hardly track how much time had lapsed since the night she was taken. Patrick was her last hope. She needed to convince Aeron to let her call him.

Before she had time to prepare a plan, the door was flung open.

"What were you doing at the Roadrunner Motel?" Aeron asked as he stomped back into the office. "I thought you were living in Georgia."

"I am," she said, stubbornly ignoring the first question, wishing she could wipe the tears from her face. If he was going to withhold information, so was she.

"How did you even get checked in?" he demanded.

"Like most people..." Seeing the angry set of his jaw, she dropped the rest of the sarcastic retort. She averted her gaze from his face and instead looked Aeron up and down again. The jeans he wore were clearly old, but they fit him as they should. They frayed out at his narrow hips slightly. His plain black T-shirt was snug around his pecs and biceps. She used to love walking around with him when she was in high school. The other girls would get jealous, thinking he was her boyfriend. She never said anything to dispute the rumors.

He'd been her brother's best friend all through high school and college. She couldn't deny that Aeron had aged well. That irritated her to admit, because he had always been full of himself back then. He was attractive and knew it, then and now. He'd always been friendly and helped her out when her brother was unavailable, even taking her to her sports practices or picking her up from school. Many times, Aeron had come home with her brother for family holidays and summer vacations. Aeron had never been overly chatty about his family and why he preferred Patrick's to his own, and no one had ever questioned it, at least not in her presence. They'd all enjoyed his company. There had been a few instances when she'd thought they would become more to one another. She'd even hoped for it. But that was quashed quickly.

He had been like family. This was a betrayal she'd never thought she would feel. How would her parents feel about her brother and Aeron participating in human trafficking? She could almost see the way her mother's face would crumple, the way the color would leave her.

Something didn't make sense. She racked her brain, thinking back to their college graduation. Aeron and Patrick had gone their separate ways, hadn't they? She wasn't even aware they were still speaking. Her brows furrowed as she thought back to the last time she had seen him. Why did he leave?

"I thought you were living up north in Massachusetts or New York or something." She shook her head.

"I was," he admitted, looking uncomfortable. "Some family things happened. I took care of them, and then I came back down here. I knew your brother had a few motels and asked him for a job. He obliged." The last part was said with a smirk.

When her brother opened his first motel, her parents were so proud. He'd opened a few other small businesses but stuck to the motel business for the most part. Or so she had thought. Some sort of rift had happened between her brother and her parents about two years ago. But she had no idea what it was. What if they knew about this?

The thought sent a new pang of dread through her body. They wouldn't have let this happen if they knew about it, she told herself confidently. Even if it ruined everything Patrick had worked for, they would have turned him in. Right?

She looked back into Aeron's eyes—the same ones she'd looked into when she was a teenager thinking he was one of the best men out there. She could almost make out her reflection in their depths, but she looked away, pained to think of what else she might find there.

She could feel his curious gaze on her, as if he was wondering what she was thinking about. Breaking the strained silence, he asked, "Need food? A bathroom?"

Both were deemed necessary the moment he asked. She hadn't given much thought to either until that moment. Subdued, she nodded.

Wedging the blade of a knife between her arm and the chair, he cut the zip ties and helped her to stand. His touch was gentle and caring. She hated it. She wanted to pull away from his touch. As much as she despised it, his touch still stirred something within her.

Extending her hands in front of her, she flexed her wrists to aid the circulation. She chanced a look at her hands. Her fingers were bruised and caked with blood. She'd been so overwhelmed the day before, she hadn't taken the time to examine her physical state. Instead, she focused on the girls—what they did and what they said.

"You know you can't keep taking women, right? They have lives, people that love them," she said on a harsh whisper.

His body tensed next to her, and his jaw was set in a firm line. "Trust me, I know." He led her out of the office. The room was empty, and ice-cold panic had her head whipping from side to side. Part of her had expected to see the girls in this waiting area. Sam and one of the men she didn't recognize were milling about.

A sad murmur escaped her lips. "Where are they?" she asked, trying to dart for the door. She needed to find them.

Aeron's hand wrapped firmly around her arm, and he dragged her to a hallway. At the end, Grant and another man stood in a doorway. That must be where the others are.

Trying to escape Aeron's grasp was a mistake. He tugged her back, causing her to cry out. Aeron pushed open a door and pulled her into the room behind him. The bathroom had four stalls. The walls of the stalls were the same gray as the front room. The stalls looked flimsy, like something that would be more at home in a prison. But then again, that was where she was—a prison of her brother's making. Across from the stalls was a counter hosting four sinks. An odor had her curling her upper lip. She didn't try to pinpoint its source for fear of being more disgusted.

He stepped back to block the door.

Turning to glare at him, she snapped, "I don't need help."

"I didn't offer. But now that you mention it, one of the other guys did." With a sneer, he leaned in close to her face.

A sudden rush surged through her body. It wasn't fear—not entirely anyway. She didn't want to dissect what it was, so she ignored it.

"Do you want me to go get him?" He nodded as he looked down at her crotch. "He said he'd be happy to help you with anything down there."

CHAPTER FOURTEEN
AERON, JULY 3RD

His statement made her flinch. He left out the part where he'd grabbed Grant by the shirt and slammed him against the entry door, rattling the glass in the panes. Aeron had threatened his life if he ever talked of her that way again or even thought of laying a hand on her. Thinking back on it now, he shouldn't have acted that way.

"Fuck," he mumbled under his breath, disappointed by his culpability. This situation required him to always keep his emotions in check. It had been difficult before but was even more so now that Maria was in the mix. Balling his hands into fists, he forced the emotions to recede. He released, stretching his fingers, and balled up his hands again, breathing slowly. Aeron wondered how he was going to survive these next couple days.

He could feel her curious gaze roaming over him. She knew him better than most, and if he wasn't careful, she would notice something she shouldn't. Silently, she turned away from him. If she wanted to ask about the mumbled curse she held it back. That wasn't like her—she never shied away from him when she wanted to know something. She was usually blunt. He was now the bastard who was keeping her captive and wasn't answering a single question she asked him.

Why would she think I'm going to answer any of her questions now? Guilt pressed in on him. I need to remember why I'm here.

But watching her make her way across the bathroom to one of the small stalls, he couldn't control where his mind wandered. Shaking his head, he forced the memories of teenage Maria out of his mind.

He kept himself stationed in front of the door to prevent anyone else from walking in. He didn't trust the brain-dead bastards, especially Grant, the big dumbass. Grant had despised him upon introduction. Patrick had given Aeron a top position and the most decision-making power when he arrived. This immediate high rank had rubbed Grant the wrong way because he had been part of this arrangement almost from the beginning. It would likely shock Maria to know he had not been one of the originators of this scheme. This was all Patrick.

Truthfully, he hoped his partaking in the entire situation shocked her. Her opinion of him was likely in the gutter after today, and he saw no way he would ever be able to salvage it. He wanted to explain; the words were on the tip of his tongue. The loathing and disgust in her eyes were bamboo under his nails, torture.

He sealed his lips, though. There was nothing he could say. No explanation would make him seem less villainous to her right now, especially since Patrick had ordered him to drug her with the rest. He had to maintain his distance, emotionally, at least.

She emerged from the stall, trying to cover her breasts with her arms as much as she could. He hadn't noticed before, but he was shocked with the realization she wasn't wearing a bra under the velvet velour. The thought had his dick stirring.

No wonder the others were ogling her. She always had been busty. Aeron was embarrassed to admit he'd noticed when she was still in high school. He was supposed to be like an older brother to her but couldn't help the things he noticed in his early twenties. He consoled himself by reminding himself that he was not actually her brother.

Clearing his throat, he shifted his weight from one foot to the other, hoping she wouldn't notice the semi he was sporting.

Leaning into the sink to wash her hands, she cringed as the hot water sprayed over her hands. Watching the water run red made his stomach clench. She pulled up the sleeves of her shirt and washed caked blood from her arms.

He hated that she had been closed in that trailer. He could only imagine the panic she endured. She had always been tough, and he had seen her fight through pain at sporting events. She was kicked directly in the ankle by another player during soccer. She'd limped off the field unassisted, never complaining. He remembered the bruise and swelling. Now was no different. He could see the determination on her face and the anger in her hazel eyes. But at the same time, something about her today seemed defeated. Her puffy red eyes gave away how much she'd cried.

He doubted the discovery of her brother and his best friend being involved in a human trafficking scheme helped. He wished he could explain everything to her. But he wasn't sure he could trust her—not yet.

Patrick often went through drastic measures to make sure no one knew his secret. He didn't dare tell her anything until he knew if she'd been put up to this. Her movements and reactions seemed genuine, but this would be just the kind of test Patrick would create—try to test each of the men in the ring and catch them with their pants down. Something told him Maria would never be a willing pawn, though.

The water finally ran clear. Drying her hands, she made her way back over to him. Her auburn hair was a mess of hay and snarls. She had tried to tamp it down with her damp hands but to no avail.

She stood only an arm's length away. He didn't think. Had anyone else been standing in front of him, he probably would have stopped himself. But the urge didn't allow him to think as he reached out and removed one piece of hay sticking out from her hair and brushed the mess away from her face.

Her eyes were filled with unshed tears, and he was sickened to think they were tears of fear. He couldn't stop the look of regret that passed over his face.

CHAPTER FIFTEEN
PATRICK, JULY 3RD

"Patrick," he said, bringing the damned phone to his ear, tamping down the irritation that wanted to lash out at the man on the other end of the line. This was an important day, and he didn't have time for all these calls. But this was a good customer calling, and he knew how important the man's business had been.

"That little bitch is missing," Juan said. "Is this some kind of joke?"

Patrick's jaw clenched. "What did you just say?"

"That little Asian bitch I got from you two weeks ago is missing. I talked to Tanner yesterday. His little cunt went missing too. I want some damn answers," Juan nearly shouted. He was a movie star who worked his way through women like they were Tic Tacs. So he'd wanted one on standby for whenever he needed a release between girlfriends.

"I'll check into it."

The line went dead, and Patrick's grip clenched around the receiver, mocking him with its dial tone.

There was a problem with his operation—he had a leak. Four women had gone missing from the men who had purchased them in the last couple of runs: two from homes in Vegas, one in Los Angeles, and one in Cincinnati. No one had seen these girls leave. They seemed to have just vanished. Poof. These women were purchased for thousands and were gone.

"Fuck!" Patrick ripped the desk phone from its cords and threw it across the room, denting the drywall. It clattered to the floor. This was going to have to be the last run for a while. Something was going on. He needed to get it figured out. Only in the last two runs had he heard of the women disappearing. The strangest part was they weren't located anywhere near one another. Huge fucking problem.

He'd called Dean at the motel to figure out how his sweet little sister had gotten checked into the motel. How in the hell she had seemed to pick the worst times to do anything was beyond him. Dean would be the next person to experience his rage. He would love to slam him into the wall.

He was supposed to be disposing of all Maria's things and cleaning the rooms thoroughly. If anyone knew where she was planning to stay, that would be the first place they went. He just hoped Dean would be able to keep from shitting himself if he got questioned.

The women would all be here tomorrow. There was so much he needed to do. And now, there was even more to be on his mind than just the usual to-dos.

The ants below were moving quickly to finish erecting the cubicles. Part of him wondered if these women were being taken by the other men in attendance. Are they trying to piss one another off?

Perhaps keeping their identities a secret should become a requirement. Some pompous asses liked to show off how much money they had. It worked out great for Patrick because they would jump the bidding up far higher than it needed to be in the beginning.

Scratching his chin, he began to pace. The creaking of the floor set his teeth on edge. Every sound in this place was making him more agitated. All he could hear were hammers, drills, saws, and the ticking of the clock above him. It was all too much.

Ripping the clock from its position, he slammed it into the opposite wall. Before he broke everything in this damn room, he needed to leave. Rolling his shoulders, Patrick retrieved his coat and gym duffle from the tree by his office door. Shoving his arms through the sleeves of his navy raincoat, he left his office. Stomping down the stairs, he wondered how he'd lost control.

Nearly knocking into Veronica at the base of the stairs, he told her to clean up his office. She was used to him causing destruction whenever he got frustrated. She would clean it and have anything damaged replaced by the next day—the wall would take longer than that.

The chill of the rainy afternoon did little to improve his abysmal mood as he stepped out into the mist. The club door slammed shut behind him. His usual gym was only a mile down the road, and he could use a good jog. Exercise was a sure way to get out his frustrations. Taking a calming breath, he jogged out of the fenced-in back parking lot.

Pushing himself as hard as ever, he challenged his muscles. Things were crumbling at his feet. Everything had been going well until he'd found out about Maria fucking up his life again. She'd been a constant pain since the day she was born. He found himself at the gym faster than he'd anticipated, filled with both irritation and accomplishment. He wanted to push his body as if he were pushing away the reality he was now living. He needed to make sure she was silenced, and he doubted Aeron would actually sedate her. Bastard always had a hard-on for her.

Entering the building, he shook out his jacket. He didn't go to a gym that was well known among others. He preferred to have the space to himself as much as possible. The fewer people who knew his whereabouts, the better. The gym had older equipment, but that didn't faze him. The entrance had locker rooms to the left and the offices to the right. The only entrance to the gym was through the locker rooms.

Scanning his badge, he entered the locker room. That security measure had been added after too many drug addicts were found dead in the showers. They'd often taken up residence in the locker rooms on rainy or chilly days. He relished the idea of one of those bastards approaching him today. Nothing would give him more pleasure than to beat the shit out of someone.

He located his locker and shoved his jacket into it. After changing his clothes, he walked out onto the floor of the gym. Weight benches lined one wall. Bars and weights of various sizes were available. Treadmills faced floor-to-ceiling windows that gave nothing but a view of the parking lot. Wanting a challenge, he found a deadlift bar. Placing his weights on it, he knew he had to establish some sort of plan. Either someone was fucking with his plans, or these girls were getting too bold. Either one was unacceptable. They needed to be broken if they were escaping on their own.

As he did his squats, he weighed his options. He needed to get Maria out of the middle of this shit. Her presence would only add to the stress that was pressing in on him. He would make sure to take care of her when she arrived. The four hundred pounds he was lifting pressed him into the padded floor of the old gym. Standing one last time, he let the bar drop from his hands as inspiration struck.

He was going to take care of two things at once. After changing back into the wet clothes he'd arrived in, he jogged back to the office. He was pleased to see the clock and phone remnants were already cleaned from the floor.

As he sat in his desk chair, his cell began to ring in his hand. *Just the person I want to talk to.* Rolling his eyes, he brought the phone to his ear.

"Patrick?" His father's gruff voice brought back the rage Patrick had eradicated with his exercise.

He forced a jovial voice. "Hey, Dad. I haven't heard from you in a while." It had been since Christmas. The rift between him and his parents seemed to deepen each year.

There was an awkward pause. In his father's true fashion, he jumped into the reason for his call. He never seemed to have time for small talk wherever Patrick was concerned. "Have you spoken to your sister?"

The desperation in his father's voice nearly made him laugh.

"No, I haven't. Is something wrong?" I should have become an actor. Probably make more money with less stress than this.

"She told your mother she was going to be staying at your motel a few days ago. We haven't heard from her since."

An accusatory tone, of course. Patrick took a few deep breaths, attempting to suppress the anger bolstering its way up his throat. The urge to lash out was grating at his windpipes.

"Oh, yes, I did hear that from my front-desk clerk. I was sorry I missed her," he said in as calm a voice as he could muster. "But he told me she only stayed one night and then was off again."

"So she's back on the road?"

"I guess so. I wasn't in the area," he said, playing the role of the concerned older brother. "Let me know if you hear from her."

His father thanked him and disconnected.

He needed to get his plan for Maria figured out before his father had his motel swarming with cops. This little wench was creating more and more of an issue the longer she lived.

Patrick laughed at his own thought as he called Dean. This dipshit is going to need some coaching on not acting like a total fucking idiot.

Chapter Sixteen
Hannah, July 3rd

Grant and yet another new face stood in the doorway. Grant flipped a switch on the outside wall. Bright lights nearly blinded her. She blinked quickly, willing her eyes to adjust to the sudden shift. The room they were in was completely empty. Not even a window occupied one of the walls.

"Hungry?" the man at Grant's elbow asked. He held a tray with three cups of microwave soup and three bottles of water.

Hannah couldn't stop herself from nodding. She hadn't eaten since the stale bread that had made up her terrible sandwich the day before.

The new man pointed to the wall opposite him. "Against that wall."

They helped each other up as they walked to the wall as one. He bent and placed the tray just inside the door, while Grant kept a hand on the hilt of the knife on his hip.

With the tray on the floor, the door shut, and the metallic click of the lock told them the men were leaving. They all wanted to eat. Hannah had never tasted such good tomato soup. She didn't even like tomato soup. It soothed her scratched and sore throat.

They ate in silence. The only sounds were them slurping the

contents of their soup cups. The way they all fell into line and listened sat heavily in her belly, like the foundation was building. Soon, would they easily take other commands as they were? Law? Obedience would build the structure of compliance in all of them while damaging their wills at the same time. She could see them all spiraling into the abyss of accommodating prisoners. The thought made her sit up straighter.

She was not going to mold to their wants and demands. These men could kiss her—she stopped that thought. Revolted by the images of Grant wanting to watch her get her pelvic exam, she brought the tomato soup back up to her dry lips.

"We have to try something," she said to the others.

Their eyes grew large at the thought. They'd all watched and, in part, experienced how little patience these men had when it came to them not listening. Or fighting back. She knew they couldn't be the first women who had been taken, and something deep in her soul told her they wouldn't be the last either. Unless they acted.

"Look, we have two options—become docile and obedient little puppies, or we yap and run and make a mess of everything. They don't care about us either way. And I doubt wherever we're going is going to be all that great either."

Cassidy and Kenzie appeared to be having a silent conversation. Hannah could hardly stand the anticipation. They appeared hesitant, and she hated the thought of going along like meek little sheep. They were, after all, surrounded by wolves, so she was going to be one too. Teeth bared, Hannah decided she wasn't going down without a fight.

CHAPTER SEVENTEEN
MARIA, JULY 3RD

She wanted nothing more than to be at home. She thought about trying to escape but didn't have a clue where she was. With five men hanging around, she didn't stand a chance. Any one of them could overpower her. Not a one of them would have to struggled to restrain her, except maybe the smaller older man. He didn't look nearly as imposing as the others.

Huffing, she pushed the noodles around the small bowl. The artificial cheese clumped in spots around the edges. Stabbing at it with the dull tip of the spoon, she tried to think. The sinking feeling in her stomach dove deeper. Aeron was the only thing stopping them from tossing her in with the others. She wasn't sure which place was better, but surely, being with Aeron would give her an advantage. She needed to tread lightly; she didn't know how far was wise to push him. Taking another bite of mac and cheese, she couldn't deny her intense hunger. The fact she could eat shocked her almost as much as Aeron's declaration.

"Trust me, I know." He'd said it with so much emotion, she almost believed him.

Taking a chance, she looked back into the eyes of a man she

wanted to strangle. "Where are you taking me? Why not just let me go home?"

"Maria, you know I can't just let you leave," he said, his grim gaze imploring her to understand more than she could.

How could she possibly understand something she didn't want to? She didn't want to know what made these men think this was acceptable.

"Damn it, Aeron, tell me something. My entire life is a disaster right now." She clenched the spoon in her fist. "I have a job that won't let me move up because I am a damn woman. I'm trapped in the building with you and who knows how many other men. Oh, and apparently, my brother is the ringleader of a human trafficking ring," she said, nearly hysterical.

"I already told you—I can't let you leave."

Forcing the panic down, she shakily placed the empty bowl on the table. "What is that supposed to mean?" Regardless of her efforts, she couldn't keep the fear out of her voice.

Aeron shifted in his chair uncomfortably.

She knew he could hear her fear. Not being afraid would be stupid. She knew the odds of getting out of this alive were slim. But she needed to keep Aeron close. There must still be some sliver of feeling left, or he would have left her with the others. She hated to think what was happening to them, but she hadn't heard a peep.

His eyes shot up to hers. Their blue depths looked like home, like somewhere she wished she could get lost in. No, he was not the same man. This was not the man she'd last seen.

She'd last seen Aeron at a stupid party she'd gone to after her boyfriend broke up with her. She'd known Patrick was coming but hadn't expected to see Aeron. They had just graduated college themselves four years ago, and she hadn't realized they still spent time together. Aeron had moved farther up north, and Patrick had made his way to New Mexico.

He'd surprised her not only by coming but also by bringing

her a beautiful bracelet with her birthstones lining it. The stones shone beautifully and sparkled in the light as she examined it that night. Aquamarine, March's birthstone, was also her favorite color.

"It's beautiful!" she exclaimed, throwing her arms around his neck.

He hugged her to him tightly and kissed her temple. When he placed her on the ground, their arms stayed around one another, their bodies pressed together from thighs to chest. In that moment, she knew she would never get over her feelings for him. She had loved him. She could no longer try to fool herself into thinking otherwise. She couldn't say she was a foolish teenager anymore. His blue eyes looked darker in that moment, and she wondered if he felt the same desire she was experiencing.

Letting people refer to him as her boyfriend when she was a junior and senior in high school had been wishful thinking on her part. When really close friends would comment on his attractiveness, she would laugh it off. But that was high school. She hadn't seen him in a few years, and she easily fell for the charm everyone talked about all those years before.

That night, she wasn't laughing at his handsomeness. The strong jaw, brilliant blue eyes, and perfectly styled hair were everything she wanted. Not to mention she could feel the hard, sculpted muscles of his body. The realization had sent a surge of heat throughout her body, which settled in her middle. She had almost been with him several years ago, and in this moment, all those emotions came back.

Their moment together had been interrupted by a painful slur —she'd been made to feel like a fool. She shook her head needing to remind herself the man in front of her now was not the same one she'd seen five years ago. Five years, and this is the circumstance when I see him again.

His question brought her attention back to him. "Well?" present him asked. "Can I trust you not to run?"

"Depends. How many men are outside that door?" she asked

snarkily. Well damn, probably should have kept that to myself. She was so angry and hurt, the resentment was difficult to keep out of her voice. The biting words wanted to be released, to inflict even a small portion of the pain she was feeling.

"At least four. Not one would be as kind as I have," he said, his gaze boring into her to make the meaning obvious.

Leaning in, she felt an uncomfortable fire in her middle.

"Oh, yes, because you have been so gracious." She bowed her head as if he were royalty and she were honored to be in his presence. Sitting back in her chair, she challenged him to refute her sarcasm as she raised her wrist to show the gouges from the ties. They looked worse than they felt. "I have several bruises courtesy of your cohorts."

She unzipped her hoodie and pulled it down one arm, revealing the dark imprints from Grant's beefy fingers. His jaw tensed as he looked at the bruises, but she didn't care. He obviously had no qualms about causing her pain or putting her in uncomfortable situations. So she was going to make sure he knew how much of an ass he was.

He groaned. "I don't want to tie you to that chair just to go get another water. Can I trust you or not?" he asked, backing out of her face for a moment.

"I keep promises," she stated simply. It was intended to hurt, and she was happy to see the understanding spread across his face.

The promises of a lifetime ago flashed in his eyes. "Then do I have your promise you will stay put? Since your word must be as good as gold," he countered with a devilish smile, recovering quickly.

She could have kicked herself. Why did I take that chance to make a dig at him?

Withdrawing her eyes from him, she nodded, crossing her free arm over her middle as she slouched in her chair. He closed the door on his way out, but she got a glimpse of the others. They were still together at a card table in the opposite corner. The only door she could see was closer to them than to her. Next time she was taken out of here, she was going to pay more attention to everything around her.

The sound of the door opening dragged their attention away from the cards in front of them, letting her know she had no chance of escaping without their noticing. Pulling up the leg of her pants, she examined her knees. Cuts from the hay were like having a thousand little papercuts peppering her kneecaps. She figured they were the cause of the discomfort she felt when walking, not to mention her feet, since this morning, they had been aching as she walked, likely from being barefoot since being taken from her motel room. The floor in the trailer, warehouse, and now here. She picked at the dried blood on her knees.

Since she had the space to herself for a minute or two, she could at least check out the cuts without her jailor looking her over every moment. Maria licked her index finger then rubbed at the dried patches of blood. Wiggling her foot closer to her butt, she cringed. Stretching the tender skin taut was uncomfortable.

She released some of the tension on her skin as she wiggled her heel closer to the edge of the chair. Aeron startled her as he reentered the room, holding a shopping bag and a couple more waters. She was so absorbed in her own task, she'd forgotten about him. How was that possible?

Letting her thighs fall closed on top of one another, she looked back up at him. She felt like a child getting caught doing something inappropriate.

He tossed the small gray plastic bag into the chair he had been occupying and looked down at her reddened knee. "What's wrong?"

"Nothing." She eyed the bags. "What's in the bag?"

He took a step closer to her as he frowned down at her. "No. My question first," he said in the same stern voice he used with the men earlier. He walked over to put himself between her and the table.

He was uncomfortably close. She didn't know if she was uncomfortable because of disgust or the unwanted lust surging through her body. Heat flitted across her skin. It settled in her center as he rested himself on the edge of the table. His feet spread wide, and she was surprised he could sit on the table and have his feet still touch the floor. If she tried that, she would look like a kindergartener sitting in an average-size chair.

"Hay cuts," she said simply, not trusting her voice. Surely, it would clue him in on her inner thoughts—and desires.

He extended his hand. Not entirely sure what he was looking for, she sat still, waiting for him to speak.

"Let me see," he said in a clipped voice, enunciating each word slowly. When it became obvious she wasn't going to move, he extended a hand to her and pulled her leg by the underside of her knee. Feeling extremely aware of his skin on hers, she trembled.

Chapter Eighteen

Aeron, July 3rd

Gently taking her knee in his hand, he could feel her body quaking beneath his touch. Keeping himself propped on the edge of the table, he leaned over her leg and placed it between his own. Several tiny slices covered her skin.

Placing her leg back down on the chair, he resisted the urge to squeeze her thigh reassuringly. "Let me get something to clean those." He unlocked the top drawer of the filing cabinet and pulled out the first aid kit.

"Why didn't you tell me sooner?" He furrowed his brows as he pulled her leg back to his lap. He asked the question with obvious concern and a little irritation. She was such a stubborn pain in the ass. This would be slightly easier if she had outgrown that trait. He rolled his eyes. That would have been far too easy.

"I didn't want to complain," she stated simply, lifting her chin.

He was surprised to hear her answer his question. It had been more rhetorical than anything else.

She leaned forward, probably to watch what he was doing.

"And what the hell is that?" he asked, putting himself into her space. He moved the hair away from the left side of her face. How did I not see this before?

There was a large bloody gash just inside her hairline. Her hair was matted and hung at an odd angle; he'd just assumed it was from lying in the hay.

"I fell into the side of the trailer while it was moving."

He watched her out of the corner of his eyes. Her eyes were trained on his hands and each move they made. Leaning back, he kept hold of her leg in his left hand while he flipped open the lid of the first aid kit. He removed alcohol pads and some gauze then put them down on the table next to him. He ripped open the package of an alcohol pad with his teeth.

The rise and fall of her chest increased. His eyes flickered to hers. He pinned her knee between his to release his left hand from its current responsibilities. Shaking the pad out to unfold it, he got ready to clean up her knee.

He dabbed at the area around the cuts, cleaning up the clumps of blood. Aeron felt her body release some of the tension, and a calm took over the room. The only sound was their mingled breathing.

"Were you afraid it was going to sting? Or that I wouldn't be gentle?"

"At this point, I don't know what to think," she snapped. "I've been drugged, thrown in a trailer, hauled to who knows where, and then strapped to a cot and then a damn chair." She huffed, making her knee wiggle in his grasp. "How am I to know what should be expected?"

He stretched his jaw, releasing the tension gathering there. Pressing his knees together more firmly, he shifted to get a better view of the affected area.

His normal instinct was to add levity to a situation, but this wasn't a time he could make a quip about pretending not to care. He was going to crumple under her hatred.

"Why are you doing this?" she pleaded, asking for answers he couldn't give.

He felt it best to leave the question as it was. The less she knew, the better off she would be. At this point, he doubted she had been sent in by Patrick to gain insight for him. She was far too upset about what was going on—honestly, he couldn't blame her.

"Just get it over with," she said with a resigned sigh. She gripped the arms of the chair, preparing for the sting.

Quickly and efficiently, he cleaned the entire area. He had to use two wipes on the first knee. Lowering one leg back to the floor, he lifted her other leg. Aeron pushed the hem of her pants up her leg, caressing her calf. When he got the material to her knee, she shifted in her seat to give him easier access. He hadn't told her to, and she hadn't asked. An unspoken understanding. This was the way they'd been, the way he remembered her.

He couldn't help but be impressed with how she held herself when she only flinched three times. With the table littered with the discarded wipes, he placed his hand on the underside of her right knee. As he lowered it back to the ground, he let his hand slide up the back of her thigh, stopping short of touching her center. Bringing his hand around to the top of her leg, he skimmed his hand back down her thigh. Her breathing ceased. She didn't speak as he let his hand rest on her knee for a moment longer. He wanted to be close to her body, to pull from her never-ending strength. Most women in this situation would be frantic, hysterical. But she, as usual, controlled as much of her emotions as she could. She let a few comments fly.

But who wouldn't?

The wish to continue roaming her body burned in his hand, and her skin was a taunt against his. Her warmth beneath his hand wouldn't allow him to pull away. There was a comfort there. He was mere inches from where he wanted to be. She still didn't say a thing to stop him. But she didn't say anything to encourage further exploration. Her body was stiff under his touch. After squeezing her thigh affectionately, he pulled her pantleg back into place. He stood from the table and discarded the wipes.

He wondered if she was affected by his touch the way he was.

He could feel a familiar desire burning inside him. They had come close to sleeping together once and only once. She'd pushed him away that day, and he'd never tried again.

Shaking his head, he reminded himself the gash on the side of her head was next. That would definitely lead to some flinching.

CHAPTER NINETEEN
MARIA, JULY 3RD

Maria had been holding her breath, waiting for him to release his grip on her leg. A heat was filling her middle. She was afraid if she didn't stay focused on her heartbeat, she would move the wrong way, and he would sense her desire. She focused on listening only for the thumping of her heart. His hands on her body made it begin beating in an irregular pattern—one she didn't recognize.

She hated herself for the desire coursing through her body. You hate him, she reminded herself.

She had always had a crush on Aeron. He very well knew that. He must have anyway. But she shouldn't like him anymore. She should hate him. Still, there was something about him that reminded her of the old Aeron, the one who had studied with her while she was in high school. The man that would take her wherever she wanted on weekends when Patrick refused.

She needed to stop thinking of him as the same man she'd fallen in love with all those years ago. This was not the same man. This man was dangerous for far different reasons. This man was a threat to her life and the lives of others.

"Where are you going to be taking these girls?" she asked, her voice husky. She felt on the verge of tears. She felt as if she were mourning him. All the while, he was still within reach. It was the strangest sensation. She had to lay the old Aeron to rest while she tried to find a way to work around this new, confusing man.

He took the plastic shopping bag back out of the chair and held it up. A small smile spread across his face. "We should clean that cut on your head."

"Damn it, Aeron, tell me where they are!" she shouted. She needed to get her mind back where it should be. It wasn't wise to be off galivanting through the past. This was now, and she was not going to let something happen to them when she could help them.

His features turned cold, and he tugged her out of the chair and dragged her to the bathroom. The other men were still at the card table, watching their every move.

Aeron held open the door for her until she entered. Once again, he guarded the door. As mad as she was at him, she couldn't find fault in the way he was trying to protect her from the other beasts roaming the building. Grant's gaze had been especially difficult to endure. That man was certainly one who wouldn't think twice about his actions, and that was more terrifying than anything else she had encountered before. She'd endured her fair share of catcalls over the years and men making advances purely because of how she looked, but once she said no, they would stop. He, she feared, wouldn't stop. *I will make sure I am never in a room alone with him.*

Turning on the hot water, she washed her hands. The scalding water burned all of the small cuts littering them. Wanting to wash all the filth from herself, she kept it burning hot, and she dipped her head into the basin and began wetting her hair. The water burned the sensitive skin of her scalp. She turned her head slowly to let the water run over the cut she'd sustained. She wanted to cry out and turn the water down, but she didn't. The heat intensified her desire to cleanse herself.

Keeping her head bent into the sink, she squeezed a dollop of shampoo from the plastic bag Aeron brought into the palm of her hand. After working it into a lather, she started working it through her hair, pulling the pieces of hay from the tangled mess as she went. Ignoring the pain in her fingertips, she scratched at her scalp to work the soap into her hair as best she could. Her anger needed to be released in some way, and this felt like the only option she had at the moment. She couldn't take out her rage on the men—they would only sedate her. She couldn't really take it out on Aeron because she didn't know how far she could push him now.

She watched the shampoo bubbles drip into the running water. They were tinged a sickening shade of pink. All she could picture was the other girls sleeping in the hay. With her face hidden, she allowed the tears to fall. Their heat mingled with the soap and water as she rinsed her hair. Her grief was swirling down the drain on the outside but settled in her soul. If she made it out of this, she would never be the same. She was going to learn to have a backbone—starting now.

Here she was, cleaning herself up, while someone she wasn't sure she could trust was guarding her. But at least she had something. The other girls had lost everything. They likely didn't even know why she wasn't with them. She didn't know what fate awaited them, but she feared what it was. Maria wished she could do something, anything.

She let her head hang as water and soap continued to drip from the wet strands. A wracking sob shook her entire body.

"Shhhh." Aeron's soothing voice sounded from her right side. Out of the corner of her eye, through her blurred vision, she could see Aeron standing at her elbow. "I wish I could assure you that everything would be okay," he whispered. "All I can do is promise you I will do everything in my power to keep you safe." One hand caressed her bicep, rubbing up and down.

She couldn't help but cling to his words. She needed some hope to cling to. He moved the hand from her arm to her back, resuming the up-and-down movements while still shushing her.

He took a small step away, and his hand left her body, leaving her feeling cold and alone. He'd retrieved a cup from the edge of the counter and began filling it with water. Aeron helped rinse the last of the cleanser from her hair. His touch was calming as he used his other hand to help work all the soap from various sections of her hair. Each touch sent shivers through her body.

When finished, he replaced the cup on the counter and began squeezing all the excess water from her hair. He wrapped a towel around her head. It was too small but would serve for what she needed. She choked on her tears. One look in the mirror confirmed they were bloodshot with dark bags below. She looked a mess.

"Why? Aeron, why?" Shifting her gaze to him, she watched as his jaw tensed at the question. She wasn't entirely sure what she was asking about. *Why he is part of this horrid scheme? Why he is helping me? Why did he make that promise?*

"It's complicated." He stepped away from her and took up his post at the door once again.

Resigned, she towel dried her hair as best she could. Turning away from him, she noticed the small window at the top of the wall. There was far more going on than he was telling her, and she was going to find out what.

After brushing out her hair, she placed everything into the plastic bag. Maria let herself into the farthest stall. She needed to pee. The moment gave her inspiration. Wiping, she cursed.

"What?" Aeron barked.

She swallowed. "I, ah, need a tampon or a pad," she said in a small voice. As if things couldn't get any more uncomfortable. *Is lying for a chance of escape acceptable?*

"Are you shitting me?" His steps sounded angry as he walked over to the door, his steps getting farther away. She knew she only had moments to act. Standing on the toilet seat, she reached for the latch on the window.

CHAPTER TWENTY
PATRICK, JULY 3RD

Patrick all but growled when he answered the incoming call. His phone hadn't stopped ringing in the last couple days. Someone always needed something. "What?"

"I got rid of it all."

Does he expect a parade for doing what he's told? Patrick waited him out. He knew the little fucker wouldn't be able to stand the silence. It took him longer than expected.

"Th-The police were here," Dean said with a shaky voice.

Patrick's jaw tensed. Fuck. "What did you do?"

"I-I told him she was in room seventeen. I took him to the room, gave him a tour, and told him she left yesterday morning at checkout time."

Patrick nodded as he listened, regardless of the fact that Dean couldn't see him. The nod was more of a way for him to help process the words, to visualize what would have gone down. His damn father must have reported Maria missing. Cops poking around at one of his destinations was the last thing he needed.

Patrick clenched his jaw at the way the kid must have acted while the cops were there. Knowing the kid, he'd probably pissed his pants. The officer probably would have noticed his nerves.

This was going to be the last time Maria screwed something up for him. They would need to avoid the motel for a few runs. This would definitely put the Roadrunner Motel on the police radar.

"D-Do you?"

"Do I what?" Patrick snapped, annoyed he had missed what the little fucker said.

There was a pause while Dean did nothing more than breathe heavily into the receiver. "I asked if you think putting that girl's car near Picacho Peak was far enough. When they find it, they'll search the hiking trails for her. Throw them off, ya know?"

Patrick had to admit the kid actually surprised him. He came up with a decent idea of where to leave the car.

"Yeah, that's fine." Patrick murmured. "Anything else?" he barked.

"No. Well, actually..."

"For fuck's sake, spit it out!" Patrick pulled at his dark hair, causing it to stand on end.

"Sorry, the cop asked if we have any cameras. I told him the ones on the property are fake. Just, ya know, there to keep people from robbing us."

Patrick thought on it for a moment. The cameras were so old, they were useless. He even forgot they were there at times. "Did he believe you?"

"I think so."

"Good. Now keep your head down and your damn mouth shut. Got it?"

More heavy breathing filled the line, along with a rustling sound.

"Got it?" Patrick asked more aggressively.

"Y-Yeah, I got it."

Disconnecting the call, Patrick tossed the phone onto his desk. Running both hands through his hair, he wondered if he was going to be bald at the end of this run. Between the bitches going missing, his sister, and this new kid that was surprisingly bright while also being unbelievably stupid, he was going to drop dead of a heart attack. He had worked so hard to build his network. His clientele. He had too much to lose. And he was hell-bent on making sure he retained it all.

CHAPTER
TWENTY-ONE
HANNAH, JULY 3RD

"What are we going to do?" Kenzie asked, nursing the last of her water.

"I don't know," Hannah said. She felt like she was saying that damn phrase more than usual. They'd all finished their soup and put the empty containers on the tray by the door.

"Why..." Kenzie began.

Hannah looked at her, drawing her brows together.

Kenzie seemed to be struggling to find the words she needed. She did her best to remain patient—another thing she needed to work on. "Why do you think Jenny died?" Kenzie asked in a whisper.

"I don't know that either."

"I have an idea," Cassidy admitted, avoiding her gaze.

"What do you mean?" Hannah asked.

Cassidy shifted, rubbing one hand up and down her velvet-clad arm. "She didn't want you guys to know because she was afraid you would act differently around her." Cassidy's dark curls bobbed around her face as she shook her head.

Hannah wasn't sure what she might be shaking her head at,

but she wanted to hear what Cassidy was going to say before she interrupted.

"She had a problem with her heart. She had to have stents put in one of her arteries a few years ago."

Hannah could have been knocked over by an ant as she registered the enormity of what Cassidy was telling her. Cassidy's throat struggled as she tried to swallow. She, too, must have a lump. "Well, when she had surgery a few years ago, they were shocked at how narrow her arteries were. The surgeon told her parents if there was ever another issue, they likely wouldn't be able to operate because of this."

Kenzie's face fell into her hands. Her body shook with sobs. "She never told me."

"She was worried you guys would treat her with kid gloves, that you wouldn't want to go places with her anymore. About two months ago, she had an EKG. I think that's what it's called. Well, they found that something was wrong, and they told her that with the state of her arteries with the last surgery, they wouldn't be able to operate this time."

"Oh my god." Hannah covered her mouth with her shaking hand.

"Her parents didn't want her to go on this trip, but she begged them. She told them she needed one last big trip, then she'd stick around home for them. I promised them I'd stay by her side." Cassidy's body shook with her sobs. "I failed them."

Hannah and Kenzie wrapped Cassidy in their arms.

"You didn't fail them. There was nothing you could have done to prevent it," Hannah said, knowing Cassidy would carry this guilt with her forever. They rocked together on the floor, holding one another until their tears dried.

Even still, they clung to one another, holding their fragile hearts together as one.

"We need to do something," Kenzie said. "We need to act."

Cassidy and Hannah nodded.

"But what?" Cassidy asked through her hiccups from having cried so hard.

"I think I have an idea." Hannah's words were slow as the plan formed in her mind.

Finally hearing movement on the other side of the door, Hannah raised the tray high above her head. It was plastic, but it was the only item in the room she had that could possibly be used as a weapon. Her fingers tingled as she gripped it with all her strength. Hannah took a steadying breath and held it in her lungs.

The steps outside the door came closer as her heart raced faster and faster. Surely, it was trying to escape, to break through her ribs. The others stood behind her, ready to run.

They'd been stationed by the door for several minutes now, waiting.

When she feared she was going to pass out from holding her breath so long, she heard metal sliding over metal. Shifting her grip to ensure she was holding onto it as best she could, she was ready.

The door opened, and as Grant stepped forward, she brought the tray down with all the force she could. She cringed at the sound, while Grant grunted. She hoped he was disoriented. The tray's impact reverberated up her arms, causing a strange sensation. Holding the tray level with her chest, she charged forward. Taking advantage of his surprise, the others rushed out the door behind her. Grant recovered. Grabbing her biceps, he forced her into the wall. Gasping, she tried to regain her breath. She felt like she was wheezing like she had as a kid with asthma.

"Ya little cunt," Grant growled, pushing her against the wall with his entire body.

Hannah's mind was spinning with the lack of oxygen, and she worried she would black out. She hoped the others made it out.

Turning, she saw Aeron walking out of the bathroom she'd been taken to earlier.

He turned in time to catch Kenzie around the waist. "What the fuck is going on?" he shouted.

Cassidy had already been restrained by the unnamed man.

"Grant? Nicholas?"

"Ambush," said the man Cassidy was struggling with.

"Get those two back in the other room," Aeron snapped. "Then, Nicholas, get your ass over here."

"No, it was my fault. It was my idea," Hannah whispered against the pressure Grant was putting on her ribs. "She was just following my lead."

"Shut up!" Grant barked, shaking her. He forced her back toward the room they'd just run out of. She and Cassidy were stuffed back into the room, with the light extinguished this time. Apparently, misbehaving meant darkness.

"Sorry, Cass. I thought that might work," Hannah said. It was her turn to feel guilt. The more she thought about it, the larger it grew. It was like an old, dried-up sponge taking hold of anything in her belly, swelling around all the hope she'd had, turning it into despair. She'd concocted the plan that now had Kenzie separated from them. She worried what they were going to do, what they might do to her.

CHAPTER
TWENTY-TWO
AERON, JULY 3RD

Fucked. I am fucked. Aeron rolled his head from side to side, trying to alleviate some of the pressure that had been building since seeing Maria removed from that damn trailer. Each moment he spent with her was beginning to break him. She couldn't ruin everything he'd been working for. He wouldn't allow it.

Sighing, he reminded himself he needed to get some space between himself and Maria—physically and emotionally. She had been through hell the last twenty-four hours. Bruises covered her wrists—the irritation with himself swelled in his gut. Stepping out into the early-evening air, he wondered how he'd gotten himself into this position. Well, he didn't have to wonder. He knew exactly what had gotten him into this—or who, rather.

"How did I get here?" he whispered as he closed his eyes. Leaning against the side of the building, he wondered what his options truly were. Quitting and running away wouldn't accomplish anything. He was here for a reason, and he needed to remember that. But he was surrounded by problems. He still had feelings for a woman whom he was holding captive and who would likely never forgive everything he'd done. He was sure he had lost her. Any trust she had in him dwindled each time he refused to answer her persistent questions.

Flashes of sad hazel eyes filled his mind. How could a woman he hadn't seen in years be causing so much havoc for him? When it came to Maria, he'd never been able to hide his feelings. Patrick's instincts were immediate, as if he'd been spying inside Aeron's desires. He'd known the minute Aeron became interested in his sister. The ensuing fight was one they'd had many times over.

He ran his fingers through his hair and rested his hands at the back of his neck. He knew he had a job that needed to be done. But Maria's appearance was putting him in a difficult position. There was no way he was going to be sedating Maria. He felt like such a hypocrite. He'd allowed the others to be sedated throughout the entire process. Guilt and disgust roiled through him.

He had to weigh out all the other people on this job too. His decisions didn't only affect him. He was surrounded by other people whose lives he had a hand in. This could be an end for so many. And who knew how many more.

Focus. He needed to focus on what had brought him here and why he was doing this.

Tapping his head against the siding, he waited for the call he needed to have. It could either go really well and in his favor or dwindle his chances at freedom. Releasing a pent-up breath, he watched as the sun was beginning to set. Its light looked eerie as it forced its way between the cacti. They became shadows. Just like the men liked to do—hide in the shadows or be around the women in falsely helpful ways. He hated the mistrust he saw in Maria, and he could only imagine what the others would feel.

Feeling the vibration against his leg, he let his arms drop heavily to his sides. Sighing, he pulled his phone from his pocket.

Hoping the other men were as busy as they were supposed to be, he accepted the call. Before the caller could say anything, Aeron said, "We have two problems."

Aeron took another deep breath as he pushed his phone back into his pocket. Nothing new from Patrick.

"Aeron?" Dr. Bryne called from the doorway.

Meeting the other man's eyes, he knew in an instant there was a problem. "What the hell is happening now?" Aeron was sick of this. Nothing was going as it was supposed to. This shit was out of control, and he was going to lose his sanity.

"I couldn't find pads or tampons."

"You're all in a tizzy over menstrual supplies?" This was easy. He could deal with this no problem.

The doctor shifted from one foot to the other. "No..." He hesitated. "She climbed out the bathroom window. I went in to give her some cotton to line her underwear, but the window was open, and she was gone."

Aeron's entire body tensed. "Tell them to lock the rest back up. Send Sam and Nicholas out to help me look. You and Grant stay here." Aeron took off around the building. Just as he'd said, the bathroom window was wide open. "Maria," he growled as he took off down the road ahead.

The buildings around them were all abandoned, and he didn't figure she would be able to make it far without shoes on. Sand and gravel crunched under his shoes as he raced down the cracked asphalt. There was no way she was going to be able to make it far on this road in its condition.

Coming to an abrupt halt, Aeron examined a piece of broken asphalt sticking up. There was blood on the jagged edge. Following the drippings, he found an old warehouse with a bay door that was standing ajar. Stopping at the edge of the door, he squatted to listen. There was shuffling coming from within the building. Flinging the door open, he raced in, following the sounds.

She was groaning but still moving.

As his eyes adjusted to the darkness, he called out, "Maria, where are you?"

Her movements stilled. He continued to the back, where he thought he'd heard her. Taking each step as quietly as he could, he peeked around each stack of old pallets that were in the back. Vision finally adjusting to the darkness, he saw more blood on the floor. Staying low, he tracked her. She crouched next to another stack of pallets ahead of him. If she turned her head to the left, she would be staring straight into his eyes. Taking a step back, he snuck around to approach her from behind.

"Aeron?" Sam called from somewhere outside.

They were so far down the warehouse floor, the light being let in was worthless. He didn't answer. Sam's presence had spooked her. Maria began to back up—right into Aeron's waiting arms. She screamed when his arms closed around her middle.

Hauling her backward, he pinned her against the wall, holding her arms above her head. "Do you have any idea what you're putting in jeopardy by doing this?"

She struggled against him and spat, "I don't give a shit."

"You will cost more women their lives. Is that what you want?" he asked, tightening his grip on her wrists.

She flinched under his grip.

"Now, I am going to put you back on the ground, and we're going to go back to the medical office. Got it?"

Her small, tight nod was good enough for him.

He gripped her chin, forcing her to look at him. "Don't try this shit again."

"Fuck off," she spat with narrowed eyes.

CHAPTER
TWENTY-THREE
HANNAH, JULY 3RD

"She got out," Kenzie said as she was forced through the door and it was slammed behind her.

"Who? Are you all right?" Hannah asked, her tone betraying her panic. She moved closer, trying to make sure Kenzie was all right.

"I'm okay. Really, I am," Kenzie said. "Maria, she escaped."

"Really?" Cassidy asked, her voice small and low.

"Do you think this is all for show?" Hannah couldn't keep the irritation at Maria out of her voice. She'd thought they would be able to bond, to get to know one another. She'd wanted them all to work together, but now she was worried Maria was not one of them. She scoffed at herself, annoyed with her own distrust.

"No, no. That's why they brought me back. I guess she snuck out the bathroom window. She faked her period so they would leave her in there to find something for her."

Hope filled Hannah's chest. "Do you think they're tricking us?"

"No, I was in the bathroom with Nicholas. Dr. Bryne came in calling her name. I thought it was weird because I hadn't seen anyone since being forced in."

"Maybe she'll find us some help," Cassidy waivered.

"They're all pretty mad. Three people were going out to look for her. But maybe she'll find someone."

Hannah's heart was racing. She wanted to get out of this room. She hoped beyond all else that Maria would be bringing help back. The thought of Maria possibly being a part of this entire nightmare festered in the back of her mind. Hope was probably a foolish notion, but with all the options she had, this was likely the best. They needed to get out. Nothing they'd tried so far had amounted to anything.

Chapter
Twenty-Four
Aeron, July 3rd

Aeron marched Maria back into the office. Well, he marched, and she hobbled.

"Dr. Bryne, office now." His anger was going to get out of control if he wasn't careful. He'd never been pushed this far in his entire life. After shoving Maria down into the chair, he strapped her down. Leaning into her, he opened his mouth to speak. Thinking better of it, he clamped his mouth closed and left the office, nearly colliding with the doctor on his way out.

"She fucked up her foot."

The doctor nodded and stepped over the threshold, kneeling at Maria's feet.

"Get ready to bring the others to the bathroom, then get them ready to get back on the trailer," Aeron snapped at Sam and Grant.

They nodded. Grant opened his mouth and looked as if he were about to speak, but Aeron shot him a withering look, and his mouth closed again. Good, maybe the asshole learned something this morning.

Stomping away, Aeron flung open the door to the break room. Bracing his hands on his knees, he doubled over to catch his breath as the door closed silently behind him. His chest was tight with an ache he didn't want to examine. She was going to be the death of him. Quite literally, he feared.

His anger with Maria was shifting into something else. Understanding? Could he understand why she'd done it? She'd put everyone—everything—in danger. Taking a calming breath, he reminded himself she wasn't aware of everything that was going on. She didn't know the impact her actions could have.

Worse yet, he didn't know if he could bring himself to force her into yet another trailer. Running his hands through his hair, he considered the options. Turmoil sank into his chest. He'd promised he wouldn't put her back in the damned trailer. But she was clearly not willing to listen.

Letting out a slow breath, he formulated his own excuses for keeping her separate. He was going to keep his promise. He just hoped he wouldn't regret it.

Pushing off his knees, he straightened. "Get your shit together, Newton," he muttered to himself. Calling himself by his last name always made him think of his high school basketball coach. He was everything Aeron had wanted in a father figure. When he'd call out to Aeron by his last name, Aeron had always known what it meant: "Pull yourself together." That was what he needed to do now.

He marched back out of the break room then made sure the trailer was ready. The girls were being prepped.

"Dr. Bryne," Aeron said as the doctor made his way out to his sedan with his medical supplies. "You'll get a call tomorrow with the results from everyone's exams?"

The doctor's green eyes nearly glowed in the late-evening sun. It was a strange thing to notice about another man. But with Maria in close proximity, he seemed to be seeing everything differently. He was no longer the distant participant who could put all the deplorable shit into different boxes. The contents were getting spilled out and creating chaos in his mind.

"Yeah. Should have the results of everything by noon tomorrow." The doctor almost looked grim.

Aeron hoped the test results would reveal what he wanted. He nodded. As he did, it was as if another box tipped, and he was forced to acknowledge everything he'd ever done that he hated. "You'll drive the SUV to the Hawk Warehouse after you drop the samples off at the lab."

Chapter
Twenty-Five
Maria, July 3rd

Maria was fuming when Dr. Bryne came in to clean and wrap her foot while Aeron stomped out like a pouting toddler. The office door opened, bouncing off the wall. She was so angry, she was ready to fight with him. Spinning as far as she could in her chair, she jolted backward when she didn't see Aeron standing on the threshold. Grant sauntered in, pulling a knife from his hip. He cut the ties around her wrists, nicking her skin on each side.

She watched as blood dripped from the shallow slice. "What are you doing?" she asked, trying to hide the fear in her voice as she stumbled to her feet.

The sickening smile on his face let her know he had zero regard for her safety. He was certainly one of the men who would have preferred she be drugged and dragged around like cattle with the other girls. She would certainly not be taken to greater pastures with this man.

"Bringin' ya to the truck. Aeron sent me to git ya. Didn' want ya left behind," he said with mock sweetness. Looking her up and down, he scowled.

Trying to put distance between them, Maria tried to sidestep him. She wanted to put the chair between them. Her muscles ached as she hobbled out of reach, and any pressure on her bandaged foot sent pain radiating up her leg. The new angle gave her a better view of his face. There was anger etched into every feature. Fear forced her to think of a way to keep away from him.

He swatted the chair out of the way. She couldn't believe Aeron would send him in to get her. He'd said he would protect her. If that were the case, this was likely the last man he would send to get her, even if he was furious with her. Then again, she'd probably pushed him too far. This could be her punishment. Not wanting him to sense her fear, she tried to stand as tall as her body would allow and glare at him.

"Keep it up. Ya cuter when ya're angry." He laughed, leaning his body toward hers.

The sound had chills running over her arms. The hairs stood at attention as her body processed her situation, sensing the danger she was in. Knowing this man would do nothing but hurt her, she took a few quick steps back. Her ass collided with the table Aeron had been sitting on earlier in the day.

She hated Grant talking to her like that. Like he thought they were flirting. Like she wanted him as if they would eventually be together.

"Just wait till pretty boy ain't around to protect ya." Smacking his lips, he grabbed her upper arms and pulled her close to his chest. "He can' be 'round all the time."

She was pinned between Grant and the table. There was nowhere she could go. She should have just run instead of trying to look brave. His words were cold, and she knew the threat behind them was as real as the man before her. If he got the chance, he would take it. He would take her. His hands on either side of her hips caged her in.

Maria tried to fight against him. His grip was far too strong for her to break. His vise-like hands closed around her biceps as he forced her to spin around. He pinned her to the table with his body, pressing himself into her back. She struggled to keep the shiver of disgust from radiating across her skin. He would know it and would enjoy her discomfort. She fought him as he tried to get a grip on her wrists. Getting hold of one, he held tight to the damaged skin.

"Ya makin' me hard, sweetheart," he breathed into her ear.

If he'd only said it to make her stop struggling, it had worked. But she could feel him, the pressure of his erection in her back. She wanted to crawl across the table, to stop his body from touching hers.

"I like a challenge," he whispered, eliciting shivered bumps across her body. Taking advantage of her stillness, he thrust himself more firmly against her as he reached for her other arm, pulling it too far out in front of her as he tied her wrists together. As he tightened it, new pain ran over her, but she wouldn't let him see her flinch.

Grant took a step back from her, adjusting himself. He pulled her by the upper arm, leading her out of the office. Maria limped as quickly as she could, trying to keep up with him. Hot anger filled her cheeks from Grant putting his body on her and Aeron for sending Grant to get her. She wanted to scream but knew any reaction would be playing into his sick game.

A shot of pain reverberated up her arm as he tugged her forward. She looked up at him. The malice on his features said he was enjoying inflicting pain on her. She wished her chance at running had gone better. Men were everywhere. Defeat filled her soul.

Outside was still. There was little to no breeze on the night air. Nothing was within sight. The pain in her foot reminded her that she was unable to run again. Not yet anyway. Getting to the door, she tried to step into the cab, but without the full use of her hands, she couldn't brace herself to pull herself in. The truck had a damn lift, making it all the more difficult for her.

"Let me help ya, sweetheart." Grant placed one hand directly below her left breast and the other under her ass. A shiver surged through her body. "Like that?" he asked, shifting his grip to be more between her legs.

"Get your hands off me," she demanded through gritted teeth, trying to wriggle from his grip. Her legs burned to kick at him, to hit him anywhere she could reach.

Grant thrust her into the seat then secured her tied hands to a longer tie strapped to the underside of the seat. This would keep her hands firmly between her knees, no doubt to prevent her from trying to get the attention of passing vehicles.

The truck's lift would make it difficult for anyone to see down into the cab. Grant gave her a sadistic smile as he hovered over her. Having her hands already bound together, she couldn't do anything to stop his perusal of her body. She wanted to scratch his eyes and blind him.

She saw Aeron glaring in their direction. He was quickly closing the distance between them, angry steps carrying him along. Grant's hands were still between her legs, messing with the cord under the seat.

"What the hell are you doing, Grant?" Aeron asked, his jaw tight.

"Helpin' ya lady," he said, feigning innocence.

Aeron's jaw tensed, and he snapped, "She's not my anything!"

She couldn't stop the pang of hurt his words filled her with.

"Remember what I said earlier," Aeron growled.

If she hadn't heard his voice, she wouldn't have known he'd spoken at all. His jaw was so firmly clenched, it didn't appear to move.

The two men finished their stare down and separated after what felt like several minutes.

Grant sat directly in front of her. Grant turned his head to look back at her, anger etched into his features. Next to her was Sam, adjusting and readjusting his glasses as he waited. She wondered if Sam was as uncomfortable with the exchange as she was.

"Fuck, man." Grant's face contorted further with anger. "Ya damn glasses are fine!" He shouted after the third or fourth time Sam removed them to clean the lenses with his T-shirt.

Without a word, Sam finished the current cleansing process and slid the glasses back onto the bridge of his nose. He didn't seem to be like the others. There was a nervousness to him, and he seemed uncomfortable with everything going on around him.

Maria wondered why he was there if he was so obviously out of his element. Was he forced into this line of work?

He had sad brown eyes that didn't have the hardness like the other men's.

Aeron slid into the driver's seat. His strong, solid body filled the space ahead of her. Her shoulders relaxed slightly as relief and sadness spread through her. How could two conflicting emotions run through a person so violently? He had always represented something safe to her while she was growing up. Now, he was a mixture of that same safety and something that curdled in her belly.

She'd always counted on Aeron to pick her up or drop her off when Patrick was unavailable. Heck, she preferred Aeron over Patrick. That, of course, had changed when they went to college, but during breaks, they were there for her. Patrick usually complained if he needed to do anything, but Aeron was always willing to help. She'd never heard him complain about being in her company.

When she'd gotten her license, her parents had surprised her with a car. It was used and was several years old, but that didn't matter. That car meant freedom. Patrick had been livid when he found out their parents had bought the car for her. When he'd gotten his license, he was told he needed to work and buy himself a car. It had taken him six months to save the money. Seeing what he had to work for just be handed to Maria was a tough pill to swallow.

She'd understood his anger, and she'd tried to tell him she was sorry and that she didn't understand why their parents would do that. But he'd never listened to her side of the story. It had hurt that he had taken it out on her the next time he and Aeron had come home for a visit.

"Come on, you guys!" Maria shouted from the base of the staircase. Patrick's room and the guest bedroom were at the top of the stairs, across from one another.

Patrick and Aeron had gotten in late the night before, and she hadn't had the chance to see them yet.

"What?" Aeron called back down the stairs as he rubbed his eyes and pulled a T-shirt over his head.

The glimpse of his bare chest sent a surge of feelings through her. She had always liked him, but this was the first moment she realized she wanted to spend time with him in a different way. The pinch she felt inside her chest was odd. It made her heart rate accelerate. She was nervous. She wanted him.

"Huh?" she asked, looking back up at him.

"You just yelled for us," Patrick snapped as he came out of his room wearing a pair of sweatpants, a T-shirt, and a scowl.

Unsure, she gave her brother a small smile. "I want to show you guys my car," she said, getting more confident as she went on.

"You mean our parents' car?"

She looked back up at her brother apologetically and croaked softly, "Yeah." She didn't miss the way Aeron gave him a stern look.

"You haven't worked a day in your life, and yet you get everything," Patrick hissed.

She opened her mouth to reply but couldn't. There was no explanation. No excuse. She couldn't control the past, and she had already apologized to him. She hadn't asked for the car and hadn't been expecting to get it. She had assumed it would have been the same deal for her to get a car as it was for Patrick.

Aeron jogged down the stairs and put his arm around her shoulder. "I would love to see your car," he said, smiling down at her before giving Patrick another pointed look.

"I'll pass." Patrick crossed the hall and slammed the bathroom door behind himself.

The sound of the truck starting made Maria aware that everyone was looking at her and brought her back to her current situation. She had no idea why they all seemed to be interested in what she had to say.

"What?" she asked, looking from Aeron to Sam. She couldn't see Grant but could feel his anger emanating through the seat.

"I asked if you need anything," Aeron said through gritted teeth.

"No," she choked out, feeling emotions build up. Past and present warred. This man who had looked out for her feelings before still was. Wasn't he? How was this possible? She knew he was doing what he could, especially since everyone else wanted her in the trailer with all the other women. Sighing, she settled back into her seat as far as she could, relaxing as much as her body would let her.

The truck ride was fairly silent. The men did not seem to get along. Each time Sam did anything, Grant had something to say about it. He rolled down the window, and Grant complained. He checked his phone for what Grant deemed too many times, and Grant let him know it was ridiculous. She doubted they could get along if their lives depended on it.

Turning to Aeron, she asked him a question she had been thinking about in a whisper, "Did you call Patrick?" She'd seen Aeron on the phone earlier while Grant was shoving her into the truck.

"Yup."

"What did he say? Why didn't you let me talk to him?" she

asked still quietly, but unable to hide the dejection in her voice. They had been driving for a few hours, and she hoped the others were asleep. She saw the tension spread through his body. It started at his jaw. He eased it slightly by adjusting his grip on the steering wheel. What could cause the tension?

"Call didn't go through."

Her eyes narrowed, looking over at him. She knew he'd spoken with someone. Who it was, she had no idea. She had just assumed it was Patrick. A sickening thought struck her. Was he talking to a wife or girlfriend? She couldn't help her eyes wandering over to his left hand. There was no ring. If he's in a relationship, how could she stand his job? Looking back up to his face, she figured the other woman probably wouldn't know.

Traveling for work, she thought bitterly.

His face was set in that same irritating show of stubbornness.

"Well, can you call him again? Let me talk to him." She was pushing, but she felt if she talked to Patrick, perhaps she could do something. Still, she worried he wouldn't even consider listening to any of her thoughts. If he was involved in other trafficking businesses, maybe the others could be more lucrative. The thought of him smuggling drugs was still bitter to swallow, but it would be better than people.

"He's out of service at the moment. We'll call in a couple hours," he said testily, not taking his eyes off the road as he spoke.

Attempting to roll her shoulders, she tried to alleviate some of the irritation that was settling in her joints. Her hands were numb from the restraints, and she could hardly move. Each movement irritated the already-damaged skin. Looking down at the ties, she desperately wanted to be freed of them.

"With it being dark out"—she motioned her head to the windshield—"can you please release my hands?"

Aeron looked back at her that time, looking concernedly down at her hands bound together and strapped to the underside of her seat. She had some range of mobility but not much. Sitting up straight was difficult. Agonizing.

"I won't open the door and jump out while going"—she leaned forward and over as close to Aeron as she could—"sixty miles an hour."

"I need to get gas." He paused for a moment as if weighing this decision heavily. "If you can behave, I will release you from the restraint keeping your hands down, but I won't take the ones keeping your wrists together off."

Anger and hurt surged through her. She had nothing to bargain with to request more. She was their prisoner and could only do what they chose to let her.

He must have seen the fire in her eyes. "That's the best I can do, Maria."

She nodded, figuring that would be better than her current position. She stoically turned to face forward and stared at the lights as the town they were approaching came into better view.

They exited the highway and headed into the town. She had no idea what town they were entering or what state they were in. They had traveled almost all night the previous two nights, but she had no idea how long they'd been in the trailer each time. She had to be several hours away from the Roadrunner Motel.

Aeron signaled that they were turning into a small self-service station. Hopping out, he turned back and looked into the back seat. She had no idea if the others were asleep, but they hadn't contributed to their conversation. Still, she strongly suspected they were. Well, she hoped they were anyway.

"Need anything?" he asked.

She couldn't stop the belittling laugh that escaped her throat. "Is that a real question?" she whispered. She was wounded, physically and emotionally. With one more glance into the back seat, he closed his door. She couldn't quite place the emotion on his face. Shifting her position in the seat, she watched him in the side-view mirror.

A rush of irritation surged through her when she saw him on the phone. He was certainly talking with someone. The urge to shout was stifled only by the hoarse voice from the seat in front of her and the tug on her hair.

"So soft," Grant whispered.

Fear melted away the annoyance she'd just felt. Terror laced her blood. This cruel man would do to her whatever he wanted. He had no qualms about where they were or who might see something.

When he spoke again, she felt his breath on her face. He was twisted around in his seat, reaching between the front seats. "What else ya have that's soft?"

Tightening his grip on her hair, he pulled her head to the side. Aeron was still pumping gas, his back to them.

"Don't touch me." She enunciated each word slowly.

"Aw, come now, sweetheart."

"Grant," Sam whispered urgently.

Maria's heart rate increased when his left hand found its way to her shoulder. Panic caused a flurry of responses. Trying to pull away from his grasp, she unintentionally ripped the hair from her scalp, making her eyes water and further bruising her hands as she tried to reach the door handle.

"Don't touch me," she repeated as the pain reminded her just how trapped she was.

Sam shifted forward, looking at a loss how to help.

"Ya know you're not exactly in a position to tell me what to do." Grant sneered, pulling her hair tighter. "Wonder how ya smooth hair would feel on my stomach while ya suck me off. Ya want out of those straps so bad... I could make a deal with ya." He gave a crude laugh.

He began sliding his hand down her shoulder toward her breast. His callused palm was coarse, catching on the velour material. She couldn't let this man grope her. She struggled against his grip and the restraints again but let out a cry of pain as the bindings dug into her flesh. She didn't care, though. The pain would be worth preventing him from touching her.

"Where's pretty boy now?" he asked mockingly. The laugh died in his throat as the front door was ripped open. Grant's grip was torn from her. Aeron cracked the man's head off the doorframe, making Maria cringe. The truck shook as his head was slammed into the headrest.

Aeron had him around the throat and whispered, "This is your final warning, Grant. If I see your hand on her again, you're fucking dead."

Grant's breaths were coming in short spurts. His hands were wrapped around Aeron's forearms.

Maria leaned back, away from them both.

"You need to release him, Aeron," Sam said gently.

Maria had almost forgotten Sam was also in the truck. How had he just allowed Grant to attack her? Looking over her shoulder, she eyed him. He was as calm and reserved as ever. She reminded herself he owed her no loyalty. That lay with her brother and Aeron.

Shoving Grant deeper into the seat, Aeron whispered something to him Maria couldn't hear. Then Aeron stood and instructed Sam to swap seats with her so that Maria was behind Aeron instead. Sam got out of the truck and walked around to the front. He and Aeron stopped at the front of the truck to speak.

"This ain't over, bitch," Grant whispered from his seat as he slid out of the truck. He lit up a cigarette, and his angry puffing made her nervous.

Her door swung open, and her heart jumped into her throat. Aeron reached between her legs, where her hands were bound. Heat and awareness rippled through her. He could have cut the lower binding from the bottom. He didn't need to reach up this high, brushing the inside of her thighs, almost in a caress.

"Did you talk to my brother?"

"Couldn't get through." His eyes narrowed on her. The pressure holding her hands down was released, but she didn't lean away from him.

"I saw you talk to someone. Who else did you call then?" she challenged. She saw a mild reaction, but he covered it up quickly.

"No one. I called again, left a message." He shrugged as if it were nothing.

She knew he was lying. But she figured it was in her best interest to let it slide since it appeared he was on her side in some ways. She couldn't afford to have him angry with her—again.

When he withdrew, his hand slid down her thigh, sending shivers through her. He pointed to the seat Sam had just occupied. Maria slid across the bench seat.

There was something in his brilliant-blue eyes when he closed the door and walked back around the truck. Aeron settled back into the driver's seat. He was breathing heavily, and his hands were shaking. She wondered if it was the adrenaline or anger or if he felt the same butterflies she did. They were still running amok in her lower belly.

Maria spent the next few minutes trying to adjust her arms to relieve some of the pain lingering from her struggling. She thought she had broken the skin but couldn't see any blood in the dim lighting. The bruises would certainly become larger by morning.

Leaning close to the headrest of his seat, she whispered to him, "Thank you."

"A promise is a promise."

Burrowing into her seat, she fell asleep watching him through the rearview mirror.

CHAPTER TWENTY-SIX
AERON, JULY 4TH

Concentrating on the road was a challenge. Grant was on a fast track to finding himself on the wrong side of Aeron's anger. Aeron knew he would have a difficult time holding himself back if Grant put another hand on Maria. Thinking of the way the man had pushed her up into the cab of the truck made his jaw clench. And the way he'd had her trapped in the back seat had nearly pushed his anger to the point of no return.

Aeron kept stealing glances at Maria while she slept. He was taken back to one night he had driven her home for Patrick after they'd all been at a party together. He and Patrick were of drinking age, but Maria wasn't.

She had never been one to break rules, but for some reason, she was hell-bent on getting drunk. She was stumbling around the party with fewer articles of clothing than she'd arrived with. She'd come to the party in a skirt and oversized sweater. The sweater was missing, leaving her in a tight tank top. Instead of the skirt, she was wearing the small spandex shorts she always wore under her skirts.

His protectiveness hadn't diminished over the years. In fact, seeing the state she was in now sent him into overdrive. There was no conceivable way she would be able to get herself anywhere safely. Someone could easily take advantage of her. Blood pounded in his ears.

As he'd become more protective, Patrick had become less concerned with her well-being. Aeron had gotten angry at how Patrick would treat her. He treated her more and more like dirt as the years passed. That night, Patrick refused to take her home, laughed, and said she could stumble her way back or pick a bed to sleep in.

Aeron shoved him out of the way. The urge to punch the petty little shit raged through him. He forced his way through the crowd toward Maria then put his arm around her.

"What are you doin'?" she asked, her speech slurred.

He placed his arm around her waist and held her close to him. She didn't resist as he'd thought she might. She actually leaned into his embrace, resting her head on his shoulder. He nearly swore when he looked down and could see right down into her skimpy tank top.

She giggled when she saw where his gaze had landed.

He cleared his throat, trying to push the thoughts away, and looked around. "Taking you home. Where are your clothes?"

She didn't answer, just shrugged under his arm. Pulling her along, he wove through the other people at the party. She giggled each time she stumbled. As they made their way into the entryway, he found both her skirt and sweater draped over the arm of a couch.

"James, I need her clothes," Aeron said, motioning to the articles on the side of the chair.

"Doubtful." He shot back with a quick quirk of his brow. "She all but melted out of them when I gave her a moment of attention. So I'm sure if you tell her your sob story, she'll jump at the chance to fuck you. Girls love that sappy bad family shit."

Maria was drunk, but she appeared to be confused by what the man was saying.

"Forget it." Aeron spat back and turned Maria toward the door.

"Call me when he beats you like his old man," James shouted to Maria.

His grip tightened around her waist. It was a trap. James was just in the mood to tangle with someone. He always was when he drank. Aeron needed to keep his head about him. He was not going to be the scapegoat. Sinking to James's level would do nothing for anyone, and he didn't want to give the ass the satisfaction of a reaction.

Exiting the house, Aeron was shocked by the cold outside. His car wasn't far, but it was terribly cold, and Maria wasn't wearing much. October in Massachusetts wasn't the warmest of places.

"You need to put my jacket on." He eased his arms from the sleeves. He was wrapping it around her when a tall blonde came out.

"Sorry about him," she said with a grimace, extending Maria's clothes to them.

Aeron took them with a small incline of his head as a thank-you. He was so irritated, he didn't want to speak to anyone but Maria. Before withdrawing, she tucked her phone number into the pocket of his pants.

Eyeing her irritably, he removed the slip of paper from his pocket and handed it back to her. Turning back to Maria, he made sure the jacket was secured and lifted her into his arms. She was fading, and he didn't trust her to walk to his car.

She snuggled into the crook of his neck. He loved the feel of her warm breath on his skin. Imagining her kissing him in that spot made his dick harden. Needing to move his mind from that thought, he tried to think of something else—anything else. But his one-track mind wouldn't let the image dissipate.

He tucked her into the passenger seat of his car, secured the seat belt, and placed her clothes on her lap. He couldn't bring her back to her parents' house like this. They would be pissed, and he didn't want them to blame him. It was Patrick's fault. Patrick was the one who'd brought her to the party—why, Aeron had no idea.

"Maria?"

"Hmmm."

"Are you going to be able to get to your room without your parents waking up?"

"They're not home," she murmured. "Conference."

He had forgotten about the business conference her parents were attending in Florida this week; they'd decided to extend their stay to the entire weekend. They wouldn't be back till Sunday.

He needed to get her home then get away from her. He feared these feelings were becoming more. He was more jealous of hearing about James going after her than he was angry about James mocking his father, and the realization was startling. Pulling the lever on the side of Maria's seat, he eased it back. Reclining the seat earned him a faint smile on her lips.

Starting the car, he looked over at Maria sleeping peacefully. He knew then that he would do anything to keep her safe.

Aeron's father was a bastard who had beat him and his mother almost daily, but Aeron had promised himself from a young age that would never be him. He had a temper but would never allow himself to put his hands on someone who hadn't hit him first. Looking down at Maria, he knew he would never put his hands on her like that. He pressed a feather-light kiss to her forehead. She shivered under his lips—whether from his touch or the chill in the air, he wasn't sure.

The drive to her parents' house was quiet.

She stirred when he tried to wake her, but he figured their safest option was for him to help her into the house. Pulling her back out into his arms, he couldn't help noticing the soft, silky feel of her slender legs. Naturally, she wrapped her arms around his neck, tucking her face close to his again.

This is going to be a long walk to her room, he told himself.

But at the same time, he didn't think it would be long enough. He wanted her close.

He turned down the hall to her room. Pushing her bedroom door open, he thought it was surprisingly clean for a teenage girl. He had a cousin a few years younger, and her room was always a disaster. Maria, on the other hand, didn't have clothes scattered about the floor. The desk under the window was neat and tidy. Her bed in the center of the room was made up.

After laying her down on the edge, he carefully removed her shoes and pulled back the covers. Aeron settled her on the pillow then covered her.

Standing next to her, he shifted the hair that lay across her face, tucking it behind one ear.

Her eyelids fluttered as she looked up at him. "Lay with me," she whispered, her eyes barely staying open.

"I'll go to the spare room."

"Mmmm." She groaned in denial. "Please?" she whispered again.

"Maria, that's not a good idea," he said delicately. He knew she'd had a crush on him, but he hadn't seen her in a while and wasn't sure if she still felt that way. He certainly didn't want to find out because she had been drinking.

Harumphing, she sat up, struggling to get out of his jacket.

"I'm going to stay the night. Just not in here with you."

The way she was wiggling drew his attention down to her chest. Kneeling on the side of the bed, he helped her release her arms from the sleeves.

Folding the jacket over one arm, he placed his hand at the base of her head, guiding her back down to her pillow. He had to lean into her to lay her all the way back. He couldn't stop himself from bringing his face to hers and kissing her cheek. She smelled of alcohol, and that was the only reminder he needed. She was not in a position to accept or initiate any advances.

He eased himself up then made his way down the hall. After

retrieving her clothes from his car, he locked the house and took the stairs two at a time up to the guest room.

~

The sound of the downstairs shower woke him early the next morning. Figuring he should check on Maria, he got out of bed, slid on some shorts, and made his way down to the kitchen. Coffee first, then he would check on her.

With two coffees in hand, he made his way down to her bathroom. Knocking gently, he called out her name.

"Come in," she called. The shower had stopped while he was brewing the coffee.

Opening the door, he froze in the doorway. Standing before him, she was only wearing a towel, wet hair framing her face. The smile that spread across her features at seeing him woke him from his daze.

"Brought you a coffee." He extended one of the mugs to her.

Her hazel eyes sparkled in the early-morning light. "Thanks." She stepped forward to accept the caffeine. When her hand released the edge of the towel, it began to slide down her chest.

The raw desire surging through his body had him placing both coffees on her desk. He advanced on her as she stepped into his embrace. Their mouths met in an eager kiss.

The feel of the wet towel on his chest made him want to rip it off her. She tilted her hips to press herself against him. He was hard. Sliding one hand down her back, he gripped her ass, pressing her more firmly against him.

"I want you," she whispered then deepened the kiss.

"Me too," he choked out between reverent touches, lifting her into his arms.

He took her back to her bed and laid her on the rumpled blankets. She pulled the edges of the towel apart, exposing herself to him. His breath caught as he looked at her. A desire so strong propelled him into bed with her. Lying above her, he looked into her hazel eyes, needing to ensure none of the drunkenness was still there. When he saw nothing but her desire, he brought his mouth back down to hers. A groan of pleasure escaped when his tongue entered her mouth.

"I should have known I'd come home to you two fucking like rabbits. You've been waiting years, haven't you?" Patrick scoffed from the doorway.

Mortification filled Maria's eyes as she hastily covered herself.

"What the fuck, Patrick?" Aeron asked angrily, blocking Maria from view while she adjusted her towel.

"Just got home. Figured I'd come check on my sister," he said with mock innocence, clearly taking joy in her discomfort. "You haven't taken enough from me over the years? Had to take my best friend, too, huh?" he asked, leaning around Aeron to look at Maria. "Fucking slut," he spat as he pushed off the doorway to leave.

Aeron clenched his fists, resisting the urge to do as he'd wanted the night before. Feeling Maria shift on the bed, he turned back to her.

"You should go," Maria whispered to Aeron, not meeting his eyes, staring at a spot on his chest.

The tears he saw welling in her eyes broke something in him. "Maria, I—"

"I said go," she repeated with a quiver to her voice, turning away from him.

He hated leaving her side.

After retrieving his belongings from the guest room, he found that Patrick had left.

Raising his hand to knock on Maria's door, he paused. He could hear her crying. Figuring he'd done enough damage for one day, he left.

He'd always wondered if they would have ended up having sex if Patrick hadn't come home. He was convinced they would have.

After that, any time they were together, Maria was careful to keep space between them.

It hurt to see the longing in her eyes while also looking to her brother with what looked like fear. The man had verbally abused her through most of her teenage years. Never understanding it, Aeron had done his best to repair any damage his idiotic friend was causing.

From then on, he wasn't able to get close enough to do that. So instead of causing her additional pain, he'd stopped going to her parents' house. Looking over at her now, he wished he'd stayed in contact. He should have told her to never visit her brother's motels.

He couldn't help but wonder if she remembered their moment too. As the memory surged through him, it caused a rush of desire. He didn't deserve to feel that desire for a woman he could never have. He doubted she would be entertaining any romantic memories that would involve him.

She would never forgive the things he'd done or allowed to happen. Anger and self-loathing at the situation he'd gotten himself into wound around his soul. Like a boa constrictor, it would soon squeeze tightly enough to kill him.

Groaning, he ran a hand through his hair.

"Why do ya have such a hard-on for that bitch?"

The question caused tension to settle in his jaw. "It's Patrick's sister. Why the hell do you think?" Aeron spat back.

"Na, its somethin' more. Ya just don't have the balls to admit it. I've heard Pat talk about his sister. He hates her. Wouldn't mind me takin' care of her." Grant was sitting at an angle that allowed him to look into the back seat.

"I do mind."

"Yup. Noticed. Exactly the problem," Grant spat.

Aeron tried to concentrate on the road ahead. The sun was beginning to rise.

"We're late," Sam interjected, effectively ending their sparring match.

"Yup, noticed," Aeron replied using Grants words.

"They gonna start wakin' up," Grant muttered. "Pull over so I can get in the back with 'em."

That had been standard procedure—if a load was running late, one person got into the back to make sure they all stayed asleep. With no good excuse to deny him, Aeron pulled the truck into the lot of a rundown truck stop. Backing up, he angled the trailer door to face the dilapidated building. But this was not a trip he wanted to do this on. He didn't want Grant back there with them today.

Of all days, not today. Rolling his shoulders, he got out of the truck then made his way around to the back of the trailer. After unlatching the trailer door, he helped Grant remove a few of the bales.

"Nothing lethal," Aeron reminded him as Grant climbed into the back.

"I been at this longer, asshole," Grant shot back.

Without another word, Aeron replaced the bales in the opening of the trailer.

With a sigh of relief, he got back into the truck.

"All good, boss?" Sam asked from the passenger seat. He had switched seats but stayed in the truck to keep an eye on Maria.

With a nod, Aeron started the truck then checked on Maria. Seeing she was still asleep, he shifted into drive and took off.

"This is going to complicate things," Sam said as they pulled back onto the highway.

"I know." Aeron grimly acknowledged the dire situation they were in. There was little he could do to prevent the inevitable, but he knew what he needed to do.

Carefully merging back into traffic, Aeron noticed a police SUV pull out behind him only minutes into their drive. Checking his speed, he carefully drove just below the limit, giving no excuse to be pulled over. For five minutes, the officer stayed behind him.

Checking the mile marker, Aeron saw they had only three more miles to go.

As he let out a breath of relief, blue lights began flashing behind him.

"Shit," Aeron muttered.

Beginning to slow, he turned on his signal to pull over. His heart was racing, ramming against his ribcage. Reaching behind his seat, he tapped Maria on the leg to wake her.

"Sam, cut those ties. Maria, put this sweatshirt on." Aeron reached for the sweatshirt he had on the floor in the back. "Maria, this is very important. I need you to put that on, cover your wrists, and pretend to be asleep."

Confusion flooded her eyes as Sam removed the ties and began forcing the hoodie over her head.

"Maria," Aeron said more sternly. "Grant is in the trailer. If you so much as hint that there is anything going on in that trailer, Grant will kill that police officer and potentially some of the girls. He is armed and will do anything to avoid prison. Do you understand me?" He was being harsh with her and knew she wasn't fully comprehending what he said.

She struggled to wake up as his words began to register. "Yes," she said while nodding and forcing her arms through the sleeves.

Aeron let his wrists hang on the steering wheel as she settled herself back into her seat to pretend to be asleep.

CHAPTER
TWENTY-SEVEN
MARIA, JULY 4TH

Holding her breath, Maria waited as the police officer approached Aeron's window. She could hear the crunch of stones against the pavement. As before, she had very few options. If she drew attention to the issue, she could risk the lives of both the officer and all the other girls. Then there was the possibility of what would happen to her afterward. Would Aeron be able to continue protecting her if she did something so rash?

"Good morning, Officer," Aeron said politely, with an odd calm to his voice. "Was there an issue with my driving?"

"Morning. I am going to cut straight to the chase. What do you have in that trailer?" the officer asked.

A car whooshed past. Maria had to force herself not to flinch when it seemed a little close for comfort, and the officer's feet shuffled in the gravel as if he was coming closer to the truck.

"We've had reports of stolen horses."

"That so?" Aeron asked in a conversational manner. "Well, we don't have any horses back there. Just a bunch of hay. Delivering it to a buddy in Nevada."

Keeping her eyes closed was proving to be more difficult than she'd anticipated. The urge to speak was like the need to breathe. She wanted to save the girls, but a dead police officer would do nothing for her. And an angry Grant would do nothing good for anyone—especially not for her.

"That's quite a way to go," the officer observed.

"No doubt. I owed him one, though."

"Just to verify, why don't you open the trailer up for me? Then we can both get on our way."

"All right, Officer," Aeron said far more calmly than Maria could have managed.

Maria's breathing quickened as her heart slammed against her ribs. Should I pretend to have an emergency to get the officer to allow us to leave? But what are we leaving to? So many possibilities flooded her mind. Before she could choose a course of action, one of the truck doors was opening.

Breathing became impossible as she listened to their footsteps. She held her breath, waiting. It was going to happen any minute now. She braced herself for the sound.

The trailer door creaked open. Then there was nothing. She waited for what felt like ages. She was afraid her lungs were going to shrivel up before she would find out what was happening behind her.

And then she heard it—a resounding bang on the cool morning breeze. Maria crumpled in the seat. Her body shook with silent sobs. She was doomed. They all were. She opened her eyes only long enough to see Aeron get back into his seat. Preparing to take off, he exhaled slowly. He was so calm, it sickened her. Bile rose in her throat. It burned.

He shifted into gear without looking at her. Was he just leaving the scene of a crime? A man could be bleeding out, and Aeron was leaving him for dead.

Maria's tears dried in the tracks they made. She stared sightlessly out the window. She was hollow. She didn't think she could feel any emotion anymore.

The man she'd thought she was in love with had allowed countless deaths to happen. He'd allowed young women to be abducted and walked away from an officer of the law that was just supposed to do his job.

Her own brother was a part of the scheme. Granted, they hadn't been close since they were young, but she still couldn't believe what he was capable of. The loss hit her like a train. She'd lost two men she loved in a flash. Not physically but emotionally. She couldn't allow herself to love men who could end others' lives and wouldn't take the time to prevent a useless loss.

The painful twist in her stomach caused her to grip at the hollowness she felt, clenching her fists around the fabric of the sweatshirt. Jaw set, she resolved to do whatever she could to escape and get the others help.

The odds of her surviving, she feared, were slim. But doing nothing and allowing Aeron to drag her from place to place was doing nothing for anyone. She was only making their lives so much easier by going quietly. She would prove she had a backbone. To Aeron, to Grant, and to anyone else who got in her way.

She knew she needed to play this right. The knot in her stomach shifted into something else. Determination.

CHAPTER

TWENTY-EIGHT

HANNAH, JULY 4TH

The trailer stopped. Hannah shifted up onto her elbows. It was light outside, and she wondered if they were at their next destination. The squeak of the door opening prompted her to lie back down. Closing her eyes, she tried to fake sleep. She could try to force her way away from them when they took her out of the trailer. She needed the element of surprise.

Peering through her lashes, she watched as only a few of the bales were removed. To her utter disappointment and dismay, Grant climbed into the trailer. The bales were replaced, and the door was shut again. Hannah had been careful not to move.

The trailer had been moving only a few minutes before it slowed again. They stopped, and she strained to hear what was happening. There was a crunching outside as someone walked by the trailer.

The sound of a strange man's voice propelled her off the floor of the trailer. He introduced himself as a police officer. Hope warmed through her chest.

For a man of his size, Grant was more agile than Hannah would have expected. He had his knife at Cassidy's throat while a twisted grin spread across his features. His eyes crinkled at the edges as if this were one of life's greatest jokes.

"Make a sound, I dare ya," Grant mocked.

Cassidy was asleep, thankfully. Hannah could only imagine the fear that would be visible in her large brown eyes if she were conscious. She had to play this cool. Grant could easily kill them all before the bales were removed, and she certainly wouldn't put it past him. Wide-eyed, she shook her head at him.

Her throat was impossibly dry. She would give anything to be back on that damned beach. She would happily go sunbathing every day for a month if that meant Jenny would be back and Cassidy would survive this.

The screech of the lever on the door being removed echoed around the trailer. To Hannah's horror, Cassidy shifted. Her eyes began to flutter open. What she wouldn't give to change places with her.

Chapter
Twenty-Nine
Aeron, July 4th

Aeron was afraid he was going to crush the shifter in his grip as he put the truck into park at the Hawk Warehouse. Pulling inside this warehouse, he knew something needed to give. This was his least favorite of their locations. It was only five miles from their final destination. That thought sickened him each time he arrived. He was ready to be through with this. This was going to be the last, he swore to himself.

The corrugated steel walls hid more evil than he liked to think they could conceal. This whole building could be taken down with one rogue vehicle. One strong storm. He longed for one to take the building to the ground, crumple it on its foundation.

"Sam, take her to the office," Aeron instructed with a tip of his head.

"Got it."

He hadn't been able to look at Maria for the remainder of the drive. The thought of what could have happened made him want to lash out. He couldn't stand to see the sadness in her eyes, so like everything else, he avoided it. He didn't watch as Sam was cinching more ties around Maria's wrists. Instead, he trudged to the trailer.

Shuffling to the back of the trailer, he knew he needed to snap out of his self-loathing and self-pitying for now. He could get back to that later. Rolling his shoulders, he removed the lock from the back of the trailer.

Once the doors were opened, two men joined him to remove the bales and get the girls out of the trailer.

"Ya bastard," Grant spat as he got out. "Had to get pulled over, didn' ya?"

"You're treading a fine line, Grant. Shut your fucking mouth before I have to shut it for you," Aeron snapped, clenching and unclenching his fists at his sides.

Grant leapt over the remaining bales, getting toe to toe with Aeron. Aeron watched the other man's heavy breathing. Grant wanted this. He was looking for a fight.

"Go cool the hell off," Aeron instructed, taking a step back. He didn't need any additional excuses to beat the prick.

"That Black bitch needs her neck cleaned up." Grant ambled away.

Aeron looked into the trailer and saw blood trickling from a cut at the base of Cassidy's neck. He could have killed Grant. He wanted to. Instead, Aeron pushed his way into the trailer and pulled the girl into his arms. There was very little blood, but her terrified eyes broke him. She didn't deserve this. None of them did. Holding her close to his chest, he headed for the break room next to the office. The door was shut, and he hoped Maria was in there already. Another run-in with Grant as he was now would not be safe.

Aeron put her on the counter in the makeshift kitchen as he pulled several handfuls of paper towels from the roll. He wet them with cold water.

"Can you hold this on the cut?" he asked, leaning toward her.

She immediately pulled back, and he felt as if she had punched him in the gut. That was why he never got involved with the women. He couldn't stand to be looked at as a predator. She tentatively took the offered paper towel.

Swallowing his pride, he searched the drawers for the first aid kit he knew would be somewhere. There were no drawers in the bathroom, so supplies were always kept in the kitchen. Finding the kit, he put it on the counter at the woman's hip.

"Are you all right? Can I put a bandage on it?"

To the first question, she gave him a look that asked if he were an idiot. "Is it deep?" she asked, cringing as she spoke.

Aeron pulled the gauze from the box as he shook his head. "Not nearly what it could have been," he said, trying to put the possibility out of his mind. Grant was a bastard, and Aeron wanted him gone. He pulled an alcohol pad from the kit and cleaned the slice. It had nearly stopped bleeding, and Aeron folded the gauze and taped it to her neck.

"That should be good for now."

She started to nod then stopped. "Okay," she whispered. Her large brown eyes looked on the verge of spilling over. He couldn't handle too much crying, especially from someone he didn't know. Leading her back out to the warehouse floor, he brought her over to the other girls.

Leaving her, he went outside to clear his mind. All he could see was finding this woman dead inside the trailer rather than having a small cut across her throat. He pulled his phone from his pocket and made a call.

"What the hell happened?" he all but shouted into the phone. "I gave your guy the signal. He shouldn't have approached the..." His sentence trailed off at the sound of movement behind him.

Spinning on the spot, he saw Maria freeze where she was lowering herself from the office window. The mixture of expressions on her face was one he could not place. Confusion. Anger. Annoyance. They all flashed by so quickly, he didn't know which was current.

Taking two quick strides, he had Maria pinned between himself and the building. He saw the anger in her eyes.

Listening back to the call he was on, he found it hard to focus on the other man's words.

"Could have ended right then," the man argued.

"What did you just say?" Aeron demanded.

"If all the girls were in that trailer, we could have had everything finished then. But no, you think things need to be your way."

"You ignorant son of a bitch. Things need to be my way because I am the one that knows what's happening. Were you aware there was a man riding in the trailer? Did you know he has been worried we are being watched?" Aeron asked in a dangerous whisper.

He had been watching Maria's expression as he spoke. Her body relaxed.

When there was no response, Aeron continued, "Did you also know he said if there were any issues, he was going to kill them all?"

"Why did you let him ride in the trailer?" the man asked. "I thought you were in control of things."

"I don't have time to explain every fucking detail to you. Next time I give you or your men a signal, you better follow it." Ending the call, he leaned into Maria.

He was having a hard time focusing with the growing pressure of their bodies pressing together. The ache of lifelong longing flowed through him. The one woman he had tried his best to keep his hands off was pressed to him, waking up all the desires he always tried to suppress.

"What is going on?" she asked, tears flooding her eyes. "Aeron, I need to know exactly what your role is in all of this."

Her pleas created a hollowness in his chest. The ache to tell her everything was building with each moment they were together. But can I trust her? That was the question he knew they were both struggling with.

Could he be trusted with her life? Could she be trusted with a secret that could end his life? Neither was an easy option. Trusting on either side could result in the end for each.

"Maria," he began, pleading for her understanding, "I cannot risk telling anyone what my role is. So as far as you know, my role is exactly what you've seen."

"What I've seen?" she asked indignantly. "I have seen the man I thought I could count on for anything tie me up. I've seen him treat other women like they're nothing. I saw you walk away from a man presumably bleeding out."

"Whoa, whoa, wait, a man bleeding out?"

"I heard the gunshot," she sobbed.

"There was no gunshot, Maria."

She scowled at him. "I heard it." She stamped her foot, fighting to push him off her.

Holding her around the waist as she tried to move, taking a small step back, he spun her and pulled her back to his chest. The last thing he wanted was for her to knee him in the balls.

"There was no gunshot, damn it, Maria" He groaned as he tried to keep her in place against him. "You heard the trailer door shutting."

She stopped fighting. "What?"

"Grant didn't fire his gun at all." She was wirier than he expected, and he was winded from trying to prevent her from escaping.

Her body lost the fight, and he knew he should loosen his grip, but he refused—couldn't.

"Please tell me, because I've also seen you look at me like you love me, but how could you?" She hiccupped then continued softly. "What's more confusing is that I know you're still protecting me as you always have. You're the best chance I have at surviving this hell."

"Maria, I will tell you everything. But not now. Not today." He eased his body away from hers. With barely enough space between them for her to turn, he tipped his head to the door. "Get back inside."

He saw the flash of fight in her eyes then watched as she looked beyond his shoulders. There was nothing to see in the distance.

"Don't make me strap you to another chair, Maria." He knew the threat would make her think twice about her escape plan. "I am tired and don't have the patience for anymore bullshit right now. Get. Back. Inside." The last three words were low and slow.

Seeing she was not going to go as easily as he wanted, he gave her a slight shove toward the opening to his left. She all but stomped back into the building, arms crossed. Aeron was reminded of young Maria getting mad when he and Patrick were going somewhere she couldn't attend. With the household being just the two kids, she'd always tried to tag along with Patrick. He'd seldom let her join them, even when it was something she could easily have been a part of.

Sidling up next to her, he guided her back to the office with a little pressure on her back. Her warmth pierced the fabric and burned into his hand.

Grant looked up at them from his phone as he sat at a table in the break area. Immediate hatred filled Aeron's limbs as they begged to rearrange the smug bastard's face.

"Maria," a small blonde called from across the room. Maria tried to rush to her, but Aeron's firm grip on her upper arm steered her back to the office.

"Sit," he demanded at the doorway to the office. As soon as her ass hit the chair, he strapped her down. The glare he received in return would have broken him previously. He was getting better at being the villain in her story.

"I need some fucking sleep, and while I do, I need to know you're not going to do anything stupid. I've been awake for over twenty-four hours babysitting your ass," he snapped. He knew she wasn't the reason for the majority of his anger, but that didn't stop him from lashing out at her. Her little escape attempt was an easy cover for the multidirectional fury he was feeling. If he was asked to name what made him angry, the list would surely fill this room.

Defiantly, she turned away.

"But first, I need to find out how you got out that damn window." Trudging back out the door, he made his way down the narrow hall and found Sam holding open the swinging door that led to the bathroom for Dr. Bryne. "Lose something?" Aeron asked with an edge to his tone.

When both men looked at him with confused expressions, he knew neither knew of Maria's newest escape attempt. She could have been a mile away by now. "Maria? She wasn't strapped down to a chair. I caught her trying to lower herself out yet another window." He looked to Sam, whose gaze shifted to Dr. Bryne.

Dr. Bryne's face fell as he met Aeron's eyes.

Raising his hands in surrender, Dr. Bryne said, "She said she wanted me to check on the cut on her head. She said it was tender. I left to get my bag." He lifted a small black bag in his hand. "I locked the office door when I left. I'd assumed someone would make sure the windows didn't open. I'm not used to this sort of..." The doctor trailed off as if there were no words to encompass everything he was being asked to do.

Aeron didn't know what Patrick was blackmailing this man with, but he figured the bastard hadn't been given an option.

"Yeah, it fucking opens!" Aeron barked as he began backing down the hall to the warehouse floor. The setup here was very similar to the other warehouse. It was smaller but was still sufficient for what it was used for. The office window had never been an issue before. Now, Aeron was potentially fucking up his own plans. The break room was located off the warehouse floor, while the office was between the bathroom and the hallway opening on the opposite wall. Being back on the warehouse floor, he felt marginally better once he saw the others were lying together in the corner. Each of the girls was being hooked up to receive saline. They were strapped down, legs and arms cinched to the cots they occupied. He disgusted himself.

"Ah, Aeron." The doctor shifted his weight from one foot to the other.

"Yes?" Aeron said it more aggressively than intended, but he didn't have enough in him to give a shit.

"Got the results. All the girls are clean, no STDs. Nothing irregular."

Aeron nodded once then turned to make his way back to the office. Never in his life had he wished for someone to have an STD, but with each test, he found himself hoping. Once a man claimed his purchase had an STD when she arrived, so Patrick had found himself a doctor to run tests and check over all the girls before they were sold. Not for any concern for their health but for his own selfish needs to make sure he could sell them all. If they had something, they couldn't be sold. But Aeron wasn't sure what Patrick would do with a girl who did test positive for something. With a shake of his head, he tried to clear his mind.

Stepping back into the office, he was met with a fiery look from Maria. The anger in her eyes was nothing compared to the frustration boiling beneath his skin. Locking the door, he looked over Maria's ties. Satisfied with her entrapment, he settled into the large sofa in the corner. No sooner had his head hit the pillow than he was swept up into dreams of their pasts.

"Maria, I think we need to talk about what happened."

"There's nothing to talk about," she said in a sweet voice, feigning ignorance.

"That's a lie, and you know it," Aeron whispered. Looking around at everyone at the cookout, he was trying to keep from drawing attention to them. It had been a few months since he had last seen her, when Patrick had interrupted their... almost encounter.

He hadn't talked with Patrick about it, figuring that was best. "Look," he tried again, halting when he saw the tears in her eyes.

"I cannot do this, Aeron," she said, brushing past him.

He watched her backside as she slowly climbed the stairs onto the porch and went in the side door of her parent's house. She casually swiped at her eye as she stepped through the door. Once she was inside, he glanced around the party again and locked eyes with Patrick. The smug ass saluted him with his glass, smirking as if knowing Maria was afraid to talk to him.

He knew Patrick blamed Maria for anything and everything that went awry with their family. He hated witnessing the way Patrick treated her. Aeron supposed that was one of the reasons he had always stayed around.

Looking back at the French doors centered on the porch, he contemplated following her in. The way she almost instantly started crying broke him in ways he couldn't explain and didn't want to examine. Exhaling, he tried to sidestep around the table in front of him but was blocked by a man with Maria's eyes.

"I've tried to ignore this. But you're going to have to choose," he said. "I'm not playing third wheel while you two get your fill of each other." Patrick grabbed a beer and drained it.

"Why does it bother you so much?"

Patrick's eyes narrowed on him. "You think I'm jealous or something?" he asked. When Aeron didn't reply, he continued. "I'm just thinking about you, man. She's a needy little pain in the ass. She'd probably get herself pregnant just to trap you."

Aeron rolled his eyes as he bent to follow Patrick's lead. He plucked a beer out of the cooler and sipped it. He doubted Maria would do such a thing, but he definitely didn't want children. Ever.

Growing up with an abusive alcoholic, he'd always been careful about both his alcohol consumption and relationships. Alcoholism could run in families. He didn't know how he would act while drunk, but he knew he didn't want to find out at another's expense. One or two—that was his limit. Before saying something he might regret, he clapped Patrick on the shoulder and tipped his head in the direction of Patrick's father. "I'm going to help your dad with the grill."

Aeron meandered around the party, talking easily with the surrogate family he'd always wished he were part of. Patrick's parents treated him as another child, and they'd taken care of anything he needed.

That made him feel guilty when he thought about his feelings for Maria. They knew about his family. Would they approve of his longing for their only daughter? Her parents treated her like a porcelain doll. He was white trash that forced people to see him how he wanted. Some had broken down the walls he lived behind, getting a glimpse of the broken boy beyond.

Nora, Patrick's mother, had patiently scratched the mortar from between those bricks until they'd all plummeted down. One night while Patrick was working in high school, Aeron had stopped by, not realizing Patrick wasn't home. He'd had a particularly violent argument with his father that had resulted in a black eye and several bruised ribs.

Nora cleaned him up and insisted he call the police. The concern in her eyes had dragged it all from him. He'd explained more to her that night than he ever had to anyone. She'd pulled him into a long hug and told him he was always welcome at their house.

This house, he reminded himself as he looked around the yard. From that night on, the spare bedroom had essentially been his. He'd never told Patrick about the conversation, and he was almost positive Nora hadn't told him either.

Reaching the grill, he looked back at the door Maria had disappeared through. Nora, with her arm wrapped around Maria's shoulders, stepped out onto the porch and whispered something in her ear. Their similarities were astounding. The shape of their eyes. Their mannerisms. The auburn hair that flowed down Maria's back matched the color of her mother's tight, short braid.

Hearing an alarm in the distance, Aeron stirred. It was the alarm he'd set on his phone. Tapping around on the table, he found his phone and deactivated the siren. Four hours.

CHAPTER THIRTY
MARIA, JULY 4TH

Having had hours to think, Maria wanted to know exactly who Aeron's cryptic phone call was with earlier. Asking him in a way that wouldn't make him ignore her was not going to be easy. Or her option was going to be to try and talk with Patrick, get some sense into him. She had to acknowledge the odds of that were slim. This was madness. How could he do this to other people? Would she ever be able to convince him to end this?

Aeron's alarm had gone off only a few minutes ago. Having given him some time to wake up, she figured now was as good a time as any.

"Aeron," she called quietly, waiting for him to meet her eyes. "If I ask you just two questions, will you answer me as honestly as you can?"

His nod was slight but perceptible.

"How many women have been abducted?"

"Honestly, I don't know. If I had to guess, I would say at least a hundred. People are getting greedy." He said the last in a whisper, and she wasn't sure if he realized he'd spoken aloud.

Nodding slowly, she looked down at the ties that bound her to the chair. "Do you enjoy doing this work?" she asked almost at a whisper.

Aeron's eyes flashed quickly to hers, his expression a mixture of anger and sadness. "No."

The breath she hadn't realized she was holding escaped. She'd assumed as much from the way he treated her, but she needed to be sure. Asking about the call would have to wait. She needed to build his trust, but she knew it meant something significant for her and the others. The chance of him telling her the truth about that one was different. She thought for far too long about what that call could have been about. After all, she'd had four hours to contemplate it while he slept. Someone hadn't taken his signal. Whatever the signal was, she knew it had to do with the police officer.

"I really need to use the bathroom, Aeron."

"Oh shit." He rose from the couch and removed the ties with his utility knife.

She no longer flinched at the sight of him extending the knife to her wrist. She'd been all over with her emotions concerning him. Seesawing between trust and distrust, she found it difficult to make up her mind from one moment to the next.

When he straightened to his full height, she followed suit.

"Can I go see the girls?"

Aeron looked down his nose at her, taking far too long to ponder her simple request. "Why?"

"Why?" she scoffed. "Are you kidding me? To check on them. Do you ever have anything to do personally with the other women?"

"No." His succinct reply hit her harder than expected.

"You do nothing to keep them safe?"

"Fuck, Maria. Of course I do. I make sure there is always water at all the locations, that there is food, that they remain hydrated, and most of all, I make sure those men keep their hands off them.

Although, with this run, I have been so damn occupied with you, I haven't been able to do what I need to." He was seething when he finished.

"Oh" was all she could muster.

"But now that you mention it, putting you over with them will cure two things for me. I won't have to worry about you trying to sneak out, and I'll be able to do what I need to do while I'm here." His strong hand wrapped around her bicep, and he marched her out to the warehouse floor. "Add another cot," Aeron barked, thrusting Maria toward the hallway.

She was hurt, no more physically than she had been a moment ago, but her ego was damaged. She'd assumed he would keep her close. Protect her. She had finally pushed him too far. Glad she hadn't pushed about the phone call, she allowed him to lead her down the hall.

Aeron took her to the bathroom. Waiting just outside the stall, he paced the length of the door. The bathroom here was much like the first warehouse.

When they made their way back out to the floor of the main room, a man she thought was named Ivan dragged a cot over to the group of girls.

"Sit," Aeron barked while Ivan got ties ready to strap her down.

"IV for her?" Dr. Bryne asked.

"I don't give a shit." Aeron turned on his heel, pulling out his cell phone.

There was silence as everyone stared at Maria. Face frozen, she didn't know what to do next. She tried to swallow, but there was a lump forming. The only familiar thing she had just turned his back on her—quite literally. She had herself in a good position, and she'd screwed it all up.

Dr. Bryne looked over the gashes on the side of her head and foot, cleaned them, and gave her a sad smile. The other girls wouldn't meet her eyes. When the doctor left, she lifted her head in Hannah's direction.

"Hannah," Maria hedged.

Hannah's glare met hers.

"Did something else happen?" Maria asked, turning to get a better look at the other two girls. There was a bandage wrapped around the front of Cassidy's neck. "Oh my god, Cassidy, what happened?" She couldn't keep the panic from her voice.

"Grant," Cassidy whispered.

"Oh, Cassidy. When did this happen?"

"This morning in the trailer." Cassidy's voice was barely audible.

Maria wondered if the damage to her throat was the cause or if it was just dry.

"I woke up when the truck got pulled over. Grant was holding me up with a knife to my throat." She cringed as she spoke, and Maria couldn't deny the sadness she felt for the woman. "I was startled, so I tried to move away from him. I was so disoriented, I didn't know there was a knife at my throat until it was too late."

"I'm so sorry that happened to you, Cassidy." Wishing she could reach out to her, Maria instead tried to implore the other woman to understand her compassion for her.

"So do you help your brother with this?" Hannah asked, an edge to her tone.

Maria gaped at her. "No," she said as if a wrecking ball had swung into her chest, knocking her off balance. "I didn't know he was involved until yesterday."

"I don't know if I can believe you," Hannah said, looking away.

Maria felt like she was trying to swallow the rogue wrecking ball.

"I wanted to come out and see you guys. Check on you." Maria was at a loss. She'd never thought the girls would think she was part of her brother's horrendous plan. But looking into each of their faces, she found the truth. Aeron's special interest in her had turned her into an enemy. She had never felt more alone in her life. Kenzie hadn't spoken to her at all.

"I tried to escape, to get us all help," she said, pleading with their desire to escape.

"That's what we were told, but..." Hannah's gaze roved over her body. "Here you are."

"Do you really think I want to be here? That I would want to help them kidnap other women?" Maria shook her head at the audacity of the insinuations.

"Where were you?" Kenzie asked, surprising Maria.

"In the office, and then I rode in the truck with Aeron, Sam, and Grant." She said his name as if it left a bad taste in her mouth.

"Why?"

"I think it was because I grew up around Aeron. He must have been having a hard time watching me..." She felt terrible suggesting it. It made it sound as if she felt her life was worth more than theirs. But wouldn't anyone's family or friends do that? Wouldn't they pick those they knew over the ones they didn't?

Kenzie nodded. "I don't like it, but I get it if it's true."

Maria felt as though she were on trial, being convicted of something she'd only been witness to.

Dr. Bryne had been the only man in the room with them, and he'd stayed in the corner of the room, sitting at the card table. The cards would shuffle, then he would play what she assumed was solitaire.

The other men made their way back into the room. Sam went to the truck and pulled the trailer back out of the bay door they'd entered through. Several minutes passed while Maria wondered where he would want to go with the truck. But soon, an older-model SUV was backing into the building. It was black and simple; all the windows had a dark tint to them. Nothing about it was memorable.

The others seemed to be done speaking to her, so she lay down on her cot and tried to think of what her life should be. She should be with her parents today, getting ready to celebrate the holiday if her calculations were correct. Today was Independence Day. How fitting.

Maria drifted into an uneasy sleep. Her brief nap was abruptly interrupted when she was pulled from the cot. The movement sent pain surging through her arm, up to her shoulder. Eyes widening in fear, she looked at the hand closed around her bicep. It was large, with a tattoo creeping onto the top of the hand. It did not belong to the man she trusted. No, this hand belonged to the man she knew would end her if he got the opportunity.

Her eyes shot up to meet Grant's. The cruel joy on his face caused her stomach to flip. The other women watched with wide eyes. No one wanted to be in his company.

He was pulling her to the SUV. She tried to dig her feet in, but her bare feet were no match for the determined clip of Grant's pace.

Swatting at the hand wrapped around her arm, she pushed away from him. "Let go of me."

"I don' think so," he growled. "Next stop, ya gonna get what ya got coming." The sadistic smile spread farther across his face. She'd never seen a smile look so menacing.

"Where are we going?" she asked, fear sinking its claws into her throat. She didn't recognize her voice.

Grant laughed as he hurled her across the floor of the warehouse. As he let go of her arm, she landed hard on her hands and knees. Her fingers burned with the dirt and grime coating the floor seeping into the cuts she'd sustained in the trailer. She wanted to cry out but refused to give him the satisfaction.

Pushing herself back to her feet, she wiped her hands on her shirt and pants. Blood smeared across the surface of the fabrics. She was about to keep walking when his large hand closed around the base of her neck. His hands could easily close around her throat; the realization had her rapidly swallowing air. As she prepared for the inevitable, the hand was tightening.

She scanned the room. Where is Aeron? Leaning forward, she tested Grant's grip.

"I don' fuckin' think so," he snarled, tightening his hand further. He leaned closer to her ear, and the hairs on the back of her neck were standing at attention.

Before he could say anything more, she saw a flash of navy out of the corner of her eye. Then Aeron's fist connected with Grant's jaw. On the first hit, Grant's grip on her neck loosened enough that she stumbled forward again, nearly colliding with the small card table on the edge of the room.

"I told you—" Aeron grunted as he sent another hit to Grant's jaw. "Not to fucking touch—" After another crunch, Grant's nose was crooked at an odd angle. "Her." he ended with a shout.

Aeron's blows were delivered in such quick succession, Grant's attempts at returning Aeron's pounding was easily avoided. By this point, they'd gained the attention of all the others in the warehouse. Sam rushed over to pull Aeron off Grant. Another two men pulled at Grant's shoulders as he regained his footing.

"Get in the fucking SUV, Maria!" Aeron barked, never taking his eyes off Grant.

She hesitated only a moment before running with a clumsy limp to the vehicle. She flung open the back door and leapt into the middle row, taking the seat behind the driver. She shut the door before she looked back at the swarm of men across the warehouse. She could see Aeron saying something, but she was too far away to hear it. With the door shut, everything outside was muffled. Swallowing hard, she locked the door. Taking calming breaths, she waited. Checking on her hands, she saw new cuts now etched into the palms.

Aeron shook Sam off his arm and turned to the SUV. Their eyes connected. The windows were all blacked out, so she didn't know why she felt he could see her. But the feeling was there—that connection she'd felt to him since she was a teenager. She could feel the anger surging through him. Every movement emanated the fury he carried.

Sam caught up to him a moment later. She watched as Sam said something to Aeron. Focusing on Aeron's lips, she thought he said, "This will be Patrick's last." She couldn't make out the last word. Patrick's last what?

CHAPTER THIRTY-ONE
HANNAH, JULY 4TH

They all rode in silence, Sam on his cell phone in the front while Aeron's rigid movements navigated the roads. Hannah was next to Maria in the middle row, and Kenzie and Cassidy were in the third row of the SUV. The child safety locks were engaged—she'd already tried to open the door after they were forced inside. They were heading into a city. This she thought was odd. Aren't they afraid of being seen? But realization struck as they entered the city limits—it was the fourth of July.

She was meant to be back home with her parents. They always went on a camping trip for the Fourth. It wouldn't be mentioned as her first or favorite annual family trip, but this year, it felt monumental to miss it.

The streets were so busy, no one would give a second glance at the SUV. Cookouts, parades, and fireworks would be on the tops of people's minds.

She tried to remember the names of street signs as they went. They all flashed by, and she couldn't retain the names of any of them. Seeing one and then the next, she swore she would remember them. None stayed in her mind for long. Memorizing something had never been so difficult. Perhaps it was the longing to remember it all, the frantic way she looked from one sign to the next, that had their names dropping from her brain the moment she read the next sign.

"Where are we going?" she whispered, her voice still hoarse. She'd been rubbing her hands across the spot at the base of her neck. It was the same spot where Cassidy's cut was. She couldn't help the movement. For a strange reason, it was soothing, although it did nothing for the dryness.

Aeron's eyes shot to hers in the mirror. "The Phoenix Stage."

"I-I don't know what that is," she said slowly.

"Selective club," Sam said without looking up from his phone.

Aeron's eyes shifted to the man. Still, Sam didn't look up. Hannah could sense a strange tension between them.

Aeron's jaw tightened again before loosening to speak. "You will each be taken out of the SUV and taken to the dressing room." He spoke the directions as if he were a robot and this was a regular speech he had to give. "Do you all understand me?"

It was a question, but she wasn't sure if he was actually asking.

There was a collective nod. "Yes, I understand."

"Good," he hissed.

They arrived at a nightclub on the edge of the city. They entered a fenced-in parking lot. The fence was tall and would block anyone from seeing in. The barbed wire along the top would prevent anyone from climbing in—or out. The building itself didn't look like much. It appeared to be nothing other than an old brick building. A bay door on the side of the building was rolling up as they backed in. Hannah didn't see Aeron press any buttons, so she knew someone was watching, anticipating their arrival. The thought had anxiety swirling in her gut.

She couldn't help but wonder if anyone had reported her group missing yet. She figured her parents had on the first day she didn't respond to any of their texts or calls. Her mother had been checking in on her every other day. Considering she'd been gone for too long, and she should have been back home already, she hoped her mother would have done something about her silence.

Craning her sore neck, she saw several men standing on the dock. All wore suits, which was not what she was expecting. They stood shoulder to shoulder, hands clenched at their fronts. Once the SUV was close enough, they approached and opened the back door. It swung up. No one would see anything from above with the door blocking the way. She watched as Kenzie and Cassidy were taken first. Cassidy struggled but stopped when one of the men reached for her throat. Her body went limp.

Rage and indignation burned in the corners of Hannah's eyes. She clenched her fists, and her nails dug into her palms. She wasn't sure where the pain was emanating from—her broken hope or the nails digging into her soft flesh. Probably both, but there was nothing else she could do, and she needed an outlet for her anger. She wanted to lunge into the front seat and take Sam's phone. To call the police. To do anything. She'd been nothing but an unwilling bystander.

"This is barbaric," Maria choked out. "What happens in there?"

Aeron focused his attention on Maria as Hannah saw another man entering, preparing to remove her. "You do not want to know, Maria."

All too soon, a set of hands was pulling Hannah through the captain's chairs in the middle row and out over a folded seat in the back. Hannah tried to take hold of one of the handles above the doors. She struggled against his grip and momentum. Once the man had her inside the building, he forced her forward as another man entered the SUV. Over her shoulder, she saw him try to reach for Maria.

"Don't fucking touch her," Aeron's voice rang out.

Hannah couldn't suppress the pang of jealousy over the fact that Maria was singled out again, getting a better fate than she was likely to find in this hellhole.

Chapter Thirty-Two
Maria, July 4th

Her throat went dry as the back door to the SUV was shut by the man who had presumably entered the car to take her out. The others were already out of sight, and her fears were at an all-new threshold. Relief both filled her and evaded her at the prospect of not knowing what was going to happen to the others. Shifting forward in her seat, she leaned over the center console.

Before she had the chance to open her mouth, Aeron said, "I am not joking about this. Stay here." He slapped the center console as they pulled the SUV away from the dock, parking along the edge of the fence.

"I can't just stay here and do nothing. What is going to happen to them?" Tears were welling in her eyes. They already thought she was part of this twisted shit. She didn't want to make that worse. But she definitely didn't want to be forced into the same roles they were in.

"You will." Aeron leaned into the back, into her space.

Sam put away his phone. He was strangely distant. Getting out, he gave her a sad smile.

Icy panic ran through her veins when a hand closed around her bicep. She was dragged closer to the center console. The determination in Aeron's eyes was almost frightening. "Stay put," was all he said before pressing his lips to hers.

It was the first time they had kissed since in her room all those years ago. All the emotions of her nineteen-year-old self rushed back. Submerged in the desires again, she leaned into him, trying to deepen the kiss. But he moved away, and now she was drowning in a sea of unknowing, confusion, and longing.

Chapter
Thirty-Three
Hannah, July 4th

Hannah and the others were forced into chairs behind identical, beautifully lit vanities. There were at least two more along the wall. The lights surrounding them were twice the size of her fists. Compared to the places they'd been at, this place was high-class.

She was shaking uncontrollably. She didn't want to know what was going to await her and the others once they left this room.

A woman who looked to be barely more than skin and bones was flicking through a rack of sequin dresses. They were the gaudiest things Hannah had ever seen. Anything that made a person look like a disco ball was not something that typically caught her eye.

In the mirror, Hannah could see her look over her shoulder periodically at her and the other girls. She didn't dare make large movements. There was a man stationed to the side of each of their vanities. The man who stood between Kenzie and Cassidy's vanities seemed to be smirking, looking almost happy.

Another woman entered the room, and she all but squealed when she saw them all sitting at the vanities.

"Finally," she cried as she raced to Hannah's vanity. "This is my first time doing everyone's hair and makeup." She acted as if she were preparing everyone to be part of a bridal party. Her excitement grated on the tiny thread of control Hannah was grasping onto.

The woman at the clothing rack shot the other girl a withering glance. "Be quiet," she snapped. She pulled down a dark-blue sequined gown and brought it over to Hannah, laying the material over her shoulder.

"What the hell are you doing?" Hannah leaned away from the woman and the offending dress.

The woman stepped closer, holding the glittery material to Hannah's cheek. Hannah leaned away again, earning an irritated huff from the woman, who made some sort of hand gesture. The man at the side of her vanity stepped forward.

Nearly pressing his mouth to Hannah's ear, he said, "You don't want to behave and get ready here with the others? If that's the case, I will take you to the other dressing room. It will be just me and you, and I will personally make sure each article fits perfectly."

Hannah was frozen in fear. She hadn't even noticed the hand that gripped her hair until she tried to turn and look at him to tell him exactly what she thought. Her head was immovable.

He straightened but kept a grip on her hair. "Now, why don't you put on the nice dress Veronica here has picked out for you?"

Hannah stumbled as he pushed her to the floor. Veronica, smirking, tossed the dress at her.

Barely catching it, she looked around herself. "Where exactly am I supposed to get dressed?"

"Right here, princess," the man behind her growled. "Or like I said, I'll take you to a more private room. Just the two of us."

Hannah's gaze met Kenzie's in the mirror. She was shaking her head. They shouldn't get separated. She shouldn't walk anywhere with this man. Hating the feel of all their eyes on her, she began to remove the sweatsuit she'd been forced into. Then, after unzipping the back, she began to pull on the dress. It was far tighter than she thought it would be. The edges of the sequins dug into her skin and scratched her legs as she pulled it on.

Her legs had a couple days' stubble. Usually, she wouldn't even consider wearing a dress with her legs looking like this. But today, it didn't matter. She didn't exactly have a choice. When she got it on, the anorexic Barbie stepped behind her and roughly pulled the tops together. She zipped it up. Hannah had never felt more confined in her entire life. This felt worse than the trailer, the cot, and the small room she'd shared with the others. This was infinitely worse because they wanted something from her. No, they were taking even more from her. Her dignity. Her privacy. Everything.

When a large hand settled on her shoulder and forced her back down onto the stool, she could feel the prick of tears beginning. It was when she met the hairdresser's eyes that she knew she was giving up. The desire to fight had been dropped to the floor with the velour tracksuit. She wondered if the hairdresser saw the defeat in her eyes, because her cheeriness and smile were gone. She no longer looked like she thought this was some kind of fun adventure.

Hannah sat stock-still as the young women cleaned her hair and face, then the girl configured her hair into some elaborate updo that she never would have tried. It was beautiful, really. When her makeup and hair were both done, she didn't recognize the woman she saw in the mirror.

The eyes she saw in the mirror were empty and hollow. She didn't watch when Kenzie and Cassidy were forced into dresses as well. The same girl created beautiful updos for them as well. She was amazed by the way she was able to twist and wrap their hair. The finishing touch on each of them was a bejeweled butterfly clip.

Reaching up behind her head, Hannah felt through her hair. It was soft and smooth. And in the center, she found she, too, had a butterfly clip. She wished she would be as free as a butterfly. Fluttering from place to place. Stopping at only the most beautiful flowers. Spending her days in the gardens outside her parents' kitchen or in a sunny meadow. And in that moment, she pictured Jenny. She wanted to imagine her in a field of flowers, where she wouldn't have to worry about the heart condition Hannah had never been trusted with. She wouldn't know the pain of being forced into a dress and makeup she never wanted. In a way, she was jealous. Jenny had the freedom of being anywhere but here, while Hannah and the others were trapped.

Chapter Thirty-Four

Aeron, July 4th

Pushing his way into the office, he found Patrick sitting behind the desk. His feet were propped up on its surface. His relaxed stance was aggravating. Aeron was dealing with so much shit, he couldn't stand the lax way Patrick maneuvered the situation.

"I see you arrived with Sam," Patrick noted as he looked at the monitor on his desk, which showed nine camera views. A silent question sat between them. Sam was not supposed to be the man with him on this leg of the trip.

Aeron knew Patrick wanted to know why, but he was going to wait him out, force him to ask. Patrick always wanted people to offer up information. The silent questions were how he weeded men out. If they couldn't pick up on the question or panicked over the subtle questions, they were out. So today, Aeron was going to force him into each question. Fuck Patrick and everything he stands for.

Patrick's gaze was still transfixed on the monitor. Aeron wondered if Patrick knew his sister was in the SUV outside—the thought had dread edging its way into his mind. Another detail he was not going to offer up willingly. Looking at the monitor, Aeron saw the women were getting changed. Each was clad in a similar dress, just in varying colors.

The dress color was selected based on their complexion and hair color. They were all in varying stages of getting dressed up. One stared at the ground then looked around terrified while the others stared straight ahead, likely in shock. He couldn't help but wonder what they saw. Did they see the custom vanities and designer dresses? Were they focused on the doors, where the exits were? That wouldn't matter, though. There were men stationed outside the rooms the girls occupied at all times.

The risk of someone running away and leading the authorities back to the club would crumble everything, so the girls were heavily guarded. He watched as the small blonde felt around in her hair as she sat in front of one of the vanity mirrors. He felt a pang of guilt. He didn't even know the girl's name. Shame washed over him. Maria made sure to know each of their names. She'd spent real time with them and bonded with them. Sickness filled his middle.

Veronica touched up the girls' makeup. She was skilled and was able to bring a brightness to their lifeless faces. The girl he'd helped that morning was not interested in anything Veronica offered. She tried to bat the makeup brushes away, and he could see a tic in Veronica's jaw. The girl was pushing away, trying to look around the room, perhaps. Veronica had a short fuse. At her signal, one of the men stationed next to the vanity stepped forward, cuffing the girls' arms behind her back. He leaned into the side of her face.

This was one of Grant's favorite parts. He loved to watch them get dressed and dolled up. It gave him some sick sense of power. Aeron was just the opposite; he hated this the most. Watching the girls be forced into skimpy dresses repulsed him.

"Well, is there?" Patrick asked, pulling Aeron's attention away from the women.

"Is there what?" Aeron asked, shaking his head.

"Is there a reason Maria isn't part of that group?" Patrick asked. "I watched as each bitch was taken out of the SUV. To my utter surprise and disgust, no Maria. Unless she's dead, but if that were the case, I'm sure you would have called blubbering."

Aeron clenched his fists at his sides. "You really want your sister with the others?" Aeron asked, his disbelief and disgust evident.

"She's always been a meddling little cunt," Patrick sneered. "At least this way, she could be useful to me." His cold eyes met Aeron's. "Or did she fuck you senseless? That's how she has always tried to connect with you, isn't it?"

The urge to wipe the superior look from Patrick's face raced through his veins. "I've never fucked your sister," Aeron spat.

"Well, someone else might be interested in her dirty little cunt." Patrick laughed.

Aeron couldn't stand the thought of Maria parading around with the others. He forced his fingers to release the fists clenched at his sides. As he forced his hands to release the tension, he wanted nothing more than to give Patrick the same treatment he'd given Grant—although a broken nose probably wouldn't be enough.

"I'm going to go down to the floor, make sure everything is ready," Aeron said as he turned to leave the office.

A cruel smile spread across Patrick's face.

Aeron arrived in the auditorium to find several of the private booths were already occupied. Men of wealth and power filled the boxes. If they wanted to keep their identities confidential, they could keep the curtains closed around their box. Many of the men were married and were public figures. Most didn't want to have their escapades publicized. They wanted to avoid as many rumors as possible. The makeshift cubicles faced the stage that would, later in the night, house the dancers. But for now, it was being prepared for a different show, one that Aeron never stayed to watch. He couldn't stomach the greed and desperation of these men. They could easily get women in a different way. But they all got off on the power and the ownership they could hold over the women in their keep, forcing them into their beds and, Aeron assumed, sometimes worse.

Checking on the stage and the lighting, he found everything already set up. As he did, he looked out into the audience. He knew it was going to be far longer than he wanted before he could get Maria out of this place, away from men that would do anything they could to take whatever they wanted. Searching the space, he couldn't see Sam. He hadn't noticed him on the camera earlier either. That was strange—they had a plan.

Pretending to inspect something on the floor, he watched as a senator he knew was married with three children stood at the edge of his private box. The bastard had two daughters of his own— what would he do if one of them was taken to be part of this shit? The men milling about in the boxes disgusted him to watch. They appeared not to have a single worry about what they were about to engage in. It was as if they couldn't imagine something bad happening to them—they were untouchable.

"Fuck this," he muttered to himself. Exiting the stage, he pushed his way through the thick black curtains that hung at the edge and descended the last few steps. He turned to go down the hall to the dressing rooms. He came to a halt when he found Patrick standing there, a manic look in his eyes, as a smile slowly spread across his lips.

"You can thank Maria." He swung a heavy tray at Aeron's head, and it collided with a deafening crack. "You should have fucking listened."

Aeron stumbled back then regained his footing quickly. He pulled his arm back as he lunged forward. Swinging his fist forward, his arm halted midway through. There were two men behind him, tugging his arms behind his back. He looked over his shoulder to see who they were. As he did, Patrick swung the tray at his head again.

This time, the hit made everything go black. He stumbled

forward. The last image in his mind was of the sadness on Maria's face when he'd left her in the SUV, alone and unprotected. The confusion, the longing.

His last thought was that he failed her as all went dark around him.

"Take him up to my office. Make sure you lock the damn door." Patrick fought the urge to kick Aeron in the gut. When he asked for something to be done, it needed to be done. Not ignored. If he let Aeron survive until morning, he would be given an ultimatum. Ignoring his request to have Maria sedated was a test, which he'd failed miserably. He didn't care that Aeron had been around for most of his life. He also didn't care that the little bitch was his sister. He'd never wanted a whiny little cunt added to their family.

Judging from the way Sam had been scurrying around the club, he knew something was up. The poor old man was afraid of everything, which led Patrick to believe Maria was in the truck. He hadn't seen the man in several minutes. Perhaps he'd gone back out to keep the bitch company. Gritting his teeth, Patrick weighed the options of going out and grabbing her or waiting for her to leave the truck. Instead, he headed back to his office. He would watch the cameras after he ensured everything was set up.

Lights and sound had been tested. They were just about ready. This was to be his best night. He was down to three women, but that would be fine. The men in attendance tonight would drop plenty of cash to make up for the lost girl and the damn news reports he had been seeing about the four girls taken from Mexico. The lucky part was they were still searching around the resort.

Unlocking his office door, he let it swing wide, banging off the opposite wall. Aeron was sprawled out along the couch. Blood was already dried to the side of his face. Bastard deserved it. Patrick's upper lip curled with disgust at the thought of someone's blood all over his couch and pillows. He would have the couch replaced tomorrow.

Sitting in his chair, he watched the cameras, waiting for Maria to make a move. The nosey wench would never be able to stave off her curiosity. She would come sneaking in and put her nose where it didn't belong. Maybe he would have her join the show to make things up to him. After all, she did owe him. Her existence had been an inconvenience for the last time. He chuckled to himself as he pictured her lined up on stage with the others.

His eyes moved quickly from one camera to the next. Perhaps she was already out of the vehicle and in the building. All the men had been instructed to notify him if they saw movement from the SUV. One man was meant to be stationed at the upper window to watch the parking lots as always. Checking that camera, he knew Charlie was indeed where he was supposed to be—ever the vigilant sniper. Which made Patrick believe Sam was not in the SUV. He would find the skittish little shit next.

Roving to a different camera, he zoomed in on the women dressed in their bright sequined dresses. The women who were all dressed were given small snacks and something light to drink. Their bodies swayed in their new high heels as they walked around the room. He imagined that was how a small child walked when they first learned—wobbly and unsure.

Patrick's phone began to vibrate, bouncing along the surface of his desk.

"Grant."

"How's it goin', boss?" Grant huffed. His voice was off.

"You sound like shit." Patrick pointed out. His voice was more nasally than usual. Fucker better not be getting sick.

Grant expelled another groan. "Aeron broke my damn nose."

Patrick waited him out until he explained the situation. He had always been told he was an impatient person, but here he was listening to Grant's sob story about Aeron fighting over Maria. The bitch shouldn't have needed a special escort to the vehicle. She was supposed to be here in a pretty little dress. She'd ruined things for the last time—he would make sure of it. He gritted his teeth at the thought of her causing more damage than Grant and Aeron usually caused to one another on their own.

Getting rid of her would make his year. He needed to do this carefully. Each day their parents had called him looking for information on Maria, he had assured them she'd checked out, but they didn't let it drop that easily. They asked if she mentioned where else she was going to stay or if she turned up at another of Patrick's motels. The only thing his parents ever wanted to talk about was Maria. Her puny accomplishments. She was an accountant. Here Patrick was a successful business owner, and all they wanted to spout off about was her.

Bullshit. She was a manipulative... The thought dropped from his mind as inspiration struck. As he thought about his new plan, Grant was still spouting off at the mouth. Damn man never talked this much.

"Grant, I have a situation. I will call you back later." As he hung up, he retrieved one of the radios they used to communicate inside the building. "Carson," he barked.

"This is Carson," the ex-football player announced.

"I am going to need you to get my car ready. Have the new kid, Preston, take your place."

"Yes, sir."

Patrick watched as he scurried around the floor, pulling Preston from his chair in the break room. There were cameras in almost every room in this building. Patrick had picked their placement to ensure he had the best view of everyone. Sometimes, he would go down and move them just to make sure no one got too comfortable.

That was likely the problem with Aeron—he was brought on, and nothing happened to shift his comfort. The prick had gotten complacent. Still lying motionless on the couch, he felt the urge to shove his bloody form to the floor.

But he had better, more exciting things to do than to hit a man while he was down. Part of the fun was for the other person to know it was happening, so Aeron already being passed out offered little gratification. Patrick laughed to himself as he thought about the way he could easily send Aeron lower. Dropping down a few pegs was inevitable for him.

Taking the steps down to the main floor, he knew he needed to make an appearance. He was always the one to introduce the show and welcome his guests. How could he make sure they were comfortable spending thousands when they might think he didn't care about them? No, he always made his presence known and spoke with anyone who wanted to talk to him. No matter how dull their stories were, he'd perfected the art of feigning interest.

He met a few of the last to arrive as he made his way to the stage. Clenching his jaw was the only thing that prevented him from being a total ass. These men knew what time this show was going to be, and they couldn't be bothered to arrive early enough to be in their seats by the starting time. Some were repeats—they should know how Patrick felt about tardiness. Unluckily for them, Patrick never forgot a slight against him. Tardiness was, in fact, something he considered to be offensive.

As he stepped out onto the stage, the lights changed to a dimmer hue to give the stage a low glow while a spotlight was trained on him. Giving his typical introduction, he introduced himself to the newcomers and welcomed back previous customers —none by name, of course.

With his closing introduction, he stepped off the stage and

watched the first woman to walk out. She had dark hair and skin; she was quite beautiful. She wore a golden-yellow dress. Her steps were clunky and off as she struggled to make her way across the stage. Paddles rose. Men always seemed to get overexcited with the first girl. In the middle, they calmed down, and when it came to the last, they all got revved up again, not wanting to leave empty-handed. He shook his head as he thought how predictable these men were.

Making his way back to his office, his steps echoed off the walls of the stairwell. He had just begun to open his office door when his radio went off.

"Patrick."

"Go for Patrick," he said, halting in his doorway.

"She's exiting the SUV."

"On my way." Patrick turned on his heel, making his way back down the stairwell. He felt excitement pumping through his veins, racing his blood to get to all the muscles of his body.

Chapter Thirty-Six
Maria, July 4th

Sitting in the SUV was miserable. Even though the car was parked in the shade, it was ridiculously hot outside. Being forced to do nothing more than stare at her surroundings had her fingers itching to get out.

Since Aeron and Sam had gone inside, she had seen absolutely no movement. She wanted to go in. She wanted to see if she could talk some sense into her brother. Perhaps he didn't know what was going on at his hotel or this nightclub. Maybe Maria could find a phone and call him. She could tell him about everything. Something in her soul told her he knew what was happening, but she didn't want to believe it. She didn't want to let the nagging thoughts into her brain—she needed something to hold onto. True, they had never been all that close, but maybe she could talk to him and convince him this was wrong. Even as she came to her decision, she knew she was likely to be disappointed when they were finished here.

Maria dropped to the ground from the driver's seat and worked her way around the SUV. Gravel dug into the sensitive skin of her feet. She was still in pain from the gash she'd received the day before. She made her way across the parking lot and over to the bay door. It still stood slightly ajar, as if inviting her inside. Committing her mind to what she was about to do, she took a steadying breath. The door was open about a foot. Squeezing herself through the gap, she listened to the sounds from down the hall. There was little she could hear.

Once inside, she listened for sounds that might give her an idea of where the others were taken. The little she could hear did not provide answers. Then she heard laughter. A woman's laughter. She followed the sounds.

Tentatively, she took the stairs. The soft music became louder with each step. What she found was more than she'd thought she would see. Cassidy was walking around the edge of a large stage. Walking was far too generous a word—she was stumbling. The way her movements were slowed and disjointed made Maria want to rush to her and help her get off the stage. The others were standing at the edge of the stage, each held in place by large men. They were all wearing similar dresses. They were short halter-top sequin dresses that covered very little of the women's bodies. Disgust and anger permeated all her senses. How could anyone force another into something as heinous as this?

She had to force herself to look away from Cassidy. She needed to know what she was up against. At the base of the stage stood several large black boxes, where she could see bidding paddles rising into the air. Someone must be speaking. Pushing the door open slightly, she listened.

An auctioneer threw out some of the most astounding dollar amounts she could have thought of. Someone's paddle rose high in the air as the auctioneer announced twenty-three thousand. No one else moved. The round was over, and Cassidy, in her skimpy dress, was pulled off the stage. A large man walked her around to the booth where the winner sat. A hand extended from inside the booth, and it was like she was sucked into the depths of the black shelter.

Maria's breath caught in her throat. More than twenty thousand. She shook her head as she searched the other booths. She recognized a few of the faces. A famous actor stood outside his booth, uncaring about the others around him. He looked almost proud as he stood with a broad smile. He wasn't afraid of the others recognizing him. He was a handsome man. Couldn't he get any number of women? Why would he need to resort to this sort of acquisition?

Maria stumbled back, suppressing the bile that was fighting its way to open air, as if it were suffocating from the happenings around her. Here in this wretched club sat an actor she had thought would be amazing to meet at one time—well, she would have been happy to meet him six seconds ago, before her world shattered even further around her. She'd seen so many of his movies. Instantly, she knew she would never be able to watch any of those movies again without picturing this scene. This was far larger than she'd ever thought. If rich actors were part of this scheme, ending it was going to be more difficult than she wanted to acknowledge.

She couldn't stand being in the building. Watching.

The women were being auctioned off like cattle. The men perusing them were all wealthy and powerful. That thought made her all the more sick. Running from the acid burning up her throat, she stumbled up the stairs, tugging herself up by the railing. All of her muscles felt weakened. Sunlight was peeking through the small window at the top of the door.

Freedom, she thought as she raced up the steps. Reaching the door, she threw her weight at it, forcing the door to slam into the exterior of the building. The sound was deafening as it rang in her ears. Before she could stop herself, the contents of her stomach escaped. She braced herself on the wall by the door.

The moment she stood back to her full height, his hand was on her wrist, and she was slammed against the brick exterior. The breath was knocked out of her as the bricks ripped at her cheek.

"What do you know? What have you heard over the last few

days?" he demanded. A fire lit in his eyes as he searched her features for answers she would never give.

"Nothing that made any sense—" She wheezed, trying to regain her breath.

"I need to know exactly what you knew before you were put on that trailer Thursday night." He pressed her body more firmly into the rough exterior. He far outweighed her, and if he kept her pressed to the wall, she would surely be crushed.

"Nothing. I swear," she cried out.

The grip he had on her wrist and the way it was twisted painfully behind her back was making her eyes water in agony. The look in her brother's eyes was unrecognizable.

"Patrick, what is going on here?" she asked, her voice breaking.

"Come on, Maria. I know you're not stupid enough to have not figured it out yet." He tightened his grip on her wrist.

Letting out a cry, she tried to get out of his grasp. The skin, still tender from the ties, burned under his strong hold as she felt parts of her cheek getting pulled away by the abrasive bricks.

"What little scintillating tidbits did your dear Aeron share with you?" he asked in his mocking tone. "I've heard the two of you have been locked up in the offices at each stop. Fucking, I assume. Can't keep those legs closed, can you?"

The smile that spread across his face was one Maria had never seen. Her hand ached to slap him. This wasn't the right moment—he was unhinged. Lashing out at him now would just enrage him further. He had started resenting her in her teenage years, but what she saw in his cold eyes was much worse than the sibling irritation he had always harbored. She knew in that moment there was no way she would convince him to stop.

"I have never slept with Aeron." She looked deep into Patrick's eyes, willing him to see the truth in her own. Perhaps that would be a way to get to him—to be honest.

He let out a guttural laugh. "Let's go for a ride."

Patrick pulled her behind him into the parking lot. She nearly lost her footing as he pulled her down the step and away from the building, toward a black two-door sports car. Blood trickled down the side of her face. He shoved her into the passenger seat of the car, knocking her head off the doorframe. The headache was instantaneous.

"If your whore ass thinks you're going to run, I'll have you know I own half the cops in this city. They'll be searching for you before you make it a mile down the road." Spit flew from his mouth as he spoke. His face was contorted into unbelievable rage as a deep crimson filled all his features.

Mind still spinning, she didn't have time to react before he was in the driver's seat and shifting the car into reverse. The abrupt acceleration had her bracing herself on the dash to avoid her entire body slamming into it.

"Once again, you tried to ruin everything I have."

"Patrick, what are you talking about? I never tried to ruin anything." She winced at the pain radiating from her head down into her eyes and across the rest of her body. Everything ached. She wanted to close them but needed to focus on where they were driving to.

"Yeah, okay, perfect little Maria. Does nothing wrong, gets everything handed to her. Your life must have been so hard. Everything I worked for, you had dropped at your feet. You ungrateful little bitch."

A quick right turn forced her into the center console. As pain shot through her ribs on impact, she forced herself to contain a groan. She needed to talk him down. He's never going to listen to anything I say.

"Patrick, I want to help you, not ruin you."

With a sadistic laugh, he merged into the holiday traffic on the highway. His speed was quickly cresting eighty miles per hour, and he showed no signs of letting off the accelerator. She wanted to both close her eyes and watch to make sure they weren't going to crash. Desperately, she tried to think of something to say to ease him out of his current rage. Panic filled her mind. She couldn't think of anything to say. It was like searching for something in the densest fog she'd ever walked through—outlines to everything were getting blurred. Blinking several times, she forced her eyes back into focus. Now was not a time to succumb to the agony stealing her every thought.

Looking at her brother, she didn't recognize anything about him. His face had become so hard with hatred, she didn't know the man behind the mask. Or maybe this was the real Patrick now. Maybe what she'd seen at holidays was the mask. This was the real man he had become. His jaw was sharp and clenched, dusted with dark stubble.

"Patrick," she croaked as her throat went dry.

"Going to start blubbering to get whatever you want?" He laughed. "Sorry to say that won't be working on me. If you want to help me, tell me who Aeron has been calling. You see, he thinks he was the one in control and that I trusted him explicitly, but seeing as he went behind my back to get you, I've known for a while I couldn't fully trust him." He changed lanes without warning, forcing Maria into the window. Other drivers honked at his erratic driving. "Fucking traffic," he muttered, flipping the bird to the car behind them.

Flexing his fingers, he adjusted his grip on the steering wheel. "He didn't come to get me. I got checked into your motel, and your brute Grant took me, along with two other men."

His expression didn't change or even register that she'd spoken.

"You see, I am not stupid enough to think in my line of work that I can count on just one person to communicate. No, that is what would be stupid. I let some think they are the only one communicating with me while I have another secretly checking in with me too. It's interesting to see how their stories can conflict," he said with a wicked smile.

White-hot shock coursed through her, sending a searing shiver over her. This wasn't only going to end badly for her. Aeron was in danger too. She had no way of contacting him or warning him, because like her brother, she knew something more was going on with him. But she wasn't entirely sure what, and she certainly wasn't going to try to help him figure it out.

"So," he said, pulling her out of her own mind. "I'll ask you again, who has he been calling?"

"Patrick, I swear to you I don't know. He kept telling me he was calling you."

"Right, right. You expect me to believe that not once during your office rendezvous, he didn't confide in you?"

"No, he didn't." More panic swam against the little fight she had left in her veins, racing her to see which could make it to her heart first—to break it just that little bit more.

With another unexpected jerk of the wheel, her head slammed off the passenger window. Letting out a moan of pain, she was fearful she would black out. Blood from her cheek smeared on the glass. Another thing to make Patrick mad. Blinking rapidly, she tried to bring her world back into focus. Her vision was blurred, and her head was pounding from the concussion she was sure she was suffering from.

They were passing a gas station she recognized. They were heading back to the last warehouse; fleeting hope filled her chest. Patrick must have seen the realization on her face.

"Excited to go back?" he sneered as she felt her face slip into something she knew must show her apprehension.

"No." Her hoarse voice came out at a low whisper.

"Shame. There is someone there that would like to put you in your place. You see, he feels that you've been a bit... How should I put it? Prissy?" he asked as if she were going to respond.

"Well, Grant doesn't take well to little bitches running their mouths. He prefers their mouths to be otherwise occupied. Since you like to fuck all my other friends, I'm sure you'd be more than happy to oblige him."

Clutching the edges of her seat, she stared at his profile. "Damn it, Patrick, I have never slept with any of your friends."

Her pleading voice only brought a vicious smile to his lips.

With the warehouse in view, Maria knew she would have only a moment to act. Subtly shifting in her seat, she prepared for the inevitable stop. Resting her hand on the door as if to brace herself for the stop, she tried to clear her mind. She focused on what she needed to do, forcing any thoughts of other issues from her mind.

She flung open the door before they were at a complete stop. Her feet hadn't even hit the ground before a strong hand was tangled in her auburn hair and her head was whipped back.

"Goddamn, you really thought I didn't know what you were getting ready to do." His laugh was manic. The hand at the back of her head shifted abruptly and slammed her face into the dash. A shooting pain radiated across her face, and more hot blood seeped down her cheek just below her right eye.

Patrick pushed open his door and dragged her across the emergency brake and center console and out his door. The hairs were being torn out of her head. "You just can't help yourself, can you?"

"Patrick, you need to stop this. This can only end badly for you," she pleaded. Her voice sounded strange. There was little she was going to be able to do to convince him to stop when all her brain wanted to do was to focus on the pain—to shut down and black out. That would be far better than the abuse she was suffering. If she were passed out, that would be less she had to see firsthand. But self-preservation needed to be on the top of her list, not the unwavering pain she was feeling.

She was stumbling over her own feet as he pulled her along behind him.

"It's going to end great for both of us," he said, propelling her into the building.

Landing on her hands and knees on the concrete, she stayed on the floor as she caught her breath while her mind raced. She was having a hard time keeping herself moving. Her awareness was becoming more and more hazy as they moved. This was nothing like the drugs Grant and the others had given her. She had lost all sense of emotion as she blacked out those nights. Now, as she was wavering into the darkness, she could feel everything. Each blink utilized far too much of the little energy she had left, and she was running on fumes.

At a card table in the middle of the room sat both Grant and a man she thought was named Hank. Both men appeared to be surprised when she entered with Patrick. Apparently, Patrick hadn't informed anyone of his plans. Recovering from their surprise, they rose to their feet.

A cruel smile crossed Grant's ugly features as his swollen eyes roamed her. Even fully clothed, she felt naked in his presence. She needed to get off the floor, but her muscles didn't want to cooperate. Her arms shook at the effort of keeping herself up. Her bruised body fought against her as she willed herself to stand. Every muscle burned with the anger of what she was putting them through.

"She's all yours, Grant," Patrick called as he made his way to the hall in the direction of the bathroom.

She hadn't thought it possible, but at those words, Grant's smile grew larger. There was a change in Hank's expression too—nervousness. He hadn't spoken to her much, but he hadn't been unkind to her. She hoped he would do something.

The throbbing in her head delayed her reactions. Before she could avoid it, Grant landed an excruciating kick to her ribs.

Moaning as she rolled over onto her side, she looked up into Grants eye's, trying to plead with him.

"Wha's wrong, princess? Want some privacy, do ya?"

His large hand closed around her bicep and yanked her to her feet with such force, she thought her arm might be dislocated. Tears filled her eyes. Trying to force her legs to keep up with his pace, she stumbled as he dragged her to the office. The burning in her feet returned. She needed to keep the strain off her arm, but her efforts were useless. The pain was blinding; white-hot agony shot to every nerve ending. Her vision was blurring as she was tossed onto the couch Aeron had slept on that morning.

Landing partially on her stomach and her damaged arm, she allowed herself to release a strangled cry into the pillow. Thankfully, it muffled the sound.

She'd never wished her mind to black out. But that was all she wished for now. She wished her consciousness would succumb to the pain that was flooding her. Every extremity pulsed with each beat of her heart. She wanted to sink into the darkness at the periphery of her vision.

The room quivered with Grant's movements. Standing over her, he grabbed her other arm and flipped her onto her back with one fluid movement. Unable to stifle another groan, Maria watched the pleasure spread across his face.

"Already got ya moanin', I see."

"Go fuck yourself," she gritted out.

He raised his hand, only to drop it to her stomach. His fingers entered the waistband of her pants. "That's what yer here for, sweetheart."

The feeling of his fingers on her bare skin made her heart beat faster, and her breathing quickened. How close his hand was to her center made her recoil. Pulling her hips away from him, she forced herself to sink deeper into the cushions. She longed to curl into a ball, but the pain in her knees from her fall on the floor opposed the urge. As Grant put more pressure on the waistband of her pants, they began to descend her hips.

Panic lodged in her throat. She wanted to scream, but nothing came out.

Chapter
Thirty-Seven
Aeron, July 4th

Aeron exited the club at a run and slid into the driver's seat of the SUV. Sam slammed the passenger door only a heartbeat later.

"What does it show?" Aeron asked, pulling away from the nightclub, squealing the tires. His head was pounding, but he knew things would be worse for Maria if they didn't hurry.

"She just arrived back to the Hawk," Sam whispered as he flicked through the apps on his phone.

"Back to the warehouse?" Aeron asked. Everything in him felt heavier than ever.

"Looks like it." Sam frowned at his phone. The older man took the safety of the women as seriously as Aeron did, and he was grateful for the tracking devices Sam had begun putting in the tracksuits and the butterfly clips. Veronica insisted on having the clips, and Sam ensured she never ran out. The new trackers had been helpful lately—especially now.

Speeding down the highway, Aeron held his breath, hoping they would get there before it was too late. It was only a five-minute drive during perfect conditions, but today was not one of those days. People were all over the roads, likely the reason Patrick had selected today as an auction day. A holiday usually meant police and other law enforcement would be otherwise occupied or delayed.

"Call the others," Aeron said as he accelerated dangerously.

Patrick could be unpredictable on his best days and downright malevolent on his worst. Aeron had a feeling this was about to be one of the latter. He'd never driven so recklessly in his life. With the exit coming into view, Aeron barely applied the brakes as they sped down the ramp and turned onto the main road. Every second could prove to be deadly, especially for Maria. Patrick had always felt that Maria had received additional love and compassion when they were young, and he was jealous. From what Aeron had seen, though, Patrick pushed his parents away at each step. He figured they only doted on Maria because she let them, whereas Patrick didn't want their coddling.

With the warehouse coming into view, he pressed harder on the accelerator. The top-heavy SUV threatened to roll as he made the last corner. He gripped the steering wheel harder as he sped into the lot. Patrick's car sat close to the door. Aeron slammed the SUV into park and jumped from the vehicle without bothering to shut off the ignition.

"Aeron," Sam called after him from the edge of the building.

He didn't have time to talk strategy. He feared what he would find when he entered the building. He hoped he would find Maria safe and unharmed, but the tension growing in his core was telling him there were slim odds of that being the case. It was eerily quiet. He would rather hear Maria shouting, screaming, or fighting in some way. Sliding through the open door, he peered around the dark room. Nothing was visible other than the cots in the opposite corner, which churned the contents of his stomach each time he saw them, and the damn card table. The bay door ahead of him was closed. Fighting the urge to call out to her, he kept his back to the wall as he inched his way around the room. He made it across the exterior wall as he approached the wall with the hallway, break room, and office. Each step was careful and quiet. He wanted the element of surprise. The office door was nearly shut.

Passing the hall to the bathroom, he heard movement behind him. A pain like no other rushed through his body. Something had been slapped across his back. Stumbling forward, he turned to face his attacker. Looking back at him, he saw the eyes so similar to those of the woman he was in love with. But it wasn't her standing on the threshold. He gasped to regain the breath Patrick had tried to knock out of him.

"I fucking knew you would pick her," Patrick sneered.

Straightening as much as he could, Aeron looked the other man over. In his left hand was a chunk of wood. In his right was a gun. He'd always had a strange love for the firearm that made Aeron slightly uncomfortable in his presence. He cleaned it almost daily and talked of wishing he could use it. Today would likely be the day, and Aeron wouldn't have been surprised to see it turned on himself.

"Patrick," he began slowly, still wheezing for air. "I am not picking sides. I care about you both."

"Well, that's funny. I thought I told you to throw her in with the rest of the lot," Patrick said, tapping the barrel of the gun on his chin. "Yeah, now that I think about it, I know I fucking told you to sedate her and put her in the trailer with the rest." His voice was growing louder with each word.

"Aeron?"

He heard her whispered plea from the office. The sound of skin against skin and a whimper from her sent fire coursing through him, heating him through, down to the tips of his fingers. Looking back at Patrick, he was sickened by the joy that spread across his face. His hands balled into fists at the thought of Grant being in that damn office with her.

"She's your sister," Aeron said, the disbelief and anger in his voice seeping through.

"She's a little slut. She's getting welcomed properly by Grant," he said as he continued to grin. Aeron was surprised to see it spread further across his face. "I know you and her spent significant time in that room together." He nodded to the door that stood barely ajar. The opening was too narrow to offer a view of what was happening beyond. "Grant wanted a turn." Patrick stepped closer as Aeron backed away, getting closer to the office. "You see, Aeron, I was beginning to suspect there was something going on with you. I started not to trust you on the last run." Patrick sidestepped Aeron a few times, placing himself between Aeron and the office. His gun hand hung loosely at his side. It was likely a ploy to see if Aeron would take the bait and try to get past him.

"So I started having Grant in there keeping track of things for me too. You see, I'm not stupid enough to let someone ruin everything just because I've known you for a few years. Just like I'm not going to let some little bitch ruin everything. So instead, I'm going to let Grant ruin her." He let out a deranged chuckle.

Aeron took a step closer to Patrick. The fire settled in his fists. The urge to break every bone in Patrick's face was overwhelming. Flexing his fingers, he forced the blood to keep flowing.

"You should stay right fucking there," Patrick spat. "I do need to ask you something, though. Who were you calling when you were telling the men you were on the phone with me?" Patrick asked, anger flushing his face.

The bay door behind Patrick began to open slowly.

Meeting Patrick's eyes, Aeron shrugged.

"I'm not a fucking idiot!" Patrick shouted. "What are you trying to do? If you are threatening my business, I will kill you." He raised the barrel of the pistol, aiming directly at Aeron's face.

Aeron did his best to keep his features calm and passive. He knew Patrick got off on people's reactions and emotions. He thrived on the fear he could inflict on others.

The lack of reaction from Aeron only furthered Patrick's unbalanced state. He didn't know what was worse—the anger or the way he clearly didn't care about consequences.

Patrick's shouting was enough of a sound cover. The door behind him opened the rest of the way, and three uniformed men entered. It was beginning to get dark outside, and no additional light seeped in as they all silently filtered in. Recognizing the signals relayed to him, he blinked quickly twice. Seeing the men raise their weapons, Aeron dove into the opening of the hallway. Hitting the floor, he heard everything at once.

"Patrick Hernandez, drop your weapon," an officer shouted.

Patrick turned to face the officers marching into his building. The Hawk Warehouse was quickly being overtaken. Patrick lifted his arm, aiming his pistol at the officers. Aeron wasn't sure who fired first. There were so many shots echoing through the building, it was hard to differentiate between a new shot and a resounding echo. Aeron's ears were ringing.

Aeron heard a woman's scream. Scrambling to his feet, he stepped out of the hallway. He saw Grant standing just outside the office doorway with Maria held to his chest. She was bleeding, and her clothes were torn and hanging off her body. She was holding up the top of her pants, the waistband of which had been cut. The bastard.

Aeron didn't take time to pause and think of the consequences of what he wanted to do. Stepping forward, Aeron retrieved the pistol Patrick had dropped. It lay only inches from him. His agonized screams replaced the echoes of the gunshots. Clutching a hole in his leg, he remained on the floor. Aeron took a step closer to Grant. His back was to Aeron. The fucker held a gun to Maria's temple. He could hear her labored breathing.

"Special Agent Newton," one of the officers shouted as a warning from the opposite side of the room.

The distraction had Grant turning to see what was behind him. Realization dawned across his face slowly. The only person behind him was Aeron.

His grip on Maria relaxed slightly, and she slumped away from him.

Patrick groaned as he looked between Aeron and the other officers, seething. "You're a goddamn cop?"

"I will fuckin' kill her!" Grant shouted frantically, looking between Aeron, Patrick, and the three officers approaching him.

Maria was obviously struggling to stay on her feet. Grant shook her to force her back upright. His large arm closed under her arms and over her chest.

"Just shoot her," Patrick pressed.

"Please," she begged. Her words, barely above a whisper, pulled at the strings that had connected them for years now. The only thing he wanted in that moment was to make sure she was safe.

Grant backed himself up to the wall to stay out of easy reach. Using Maria as a shield, he kept his gaze divided between Aeron and the other officers. Aeron's blood boiled through his veins.

"Just fuckin' shoot her!" Patrick yelled from the floor.

Aeron had half a mind to beat the life out of him.

"Grant Montgomery, drop your weapon," one of the officers called from across the warehouse floor.

His face lost all color at the mention of his full name. He was beginning to realize he was effectively fucked. He was surrounded, with no escape. The other three officers took another step closer to Grant and Maria. Aeron could feel Grant's anxiety radiating throughout the room. He was getting more and more frantic as time went by.

Grant pressed Maria closer to his chest. She let out a tiny squeak.

"Ya bastard, ya're a cop?" Grant's voice was both indignant and shocked. He was holding Maria too tightly, and her head lolled to one side.

Aeron wondered if she was suffocating. Blood was running down her face. His heart was racing and ready to escape his chest. It wanted to be with Maria, begging her to be okay.

While Grant was focused on him, another of the officers took a few silent steps closer.

"I am," Aeron said slowly, hoping to keep Grant's attention on him.

But as luck would have it, he turned back to the others.

"This wasn't my idea." Grant was becoming desperate, and in Aeron's experience, desperation meant impulsivity. He shifted when he noticed the other officer was closer than before.

Maria was like a rag doll in his arms. Her blood was dripping onto the floor, creating a small pool at their feet. Aeron had to fight with everything in him not to rush at Grant. Once Grant was too busy trying to face off with the other three officers, Aeron took another hesitant step forward. Taking aim, he pulled the trigger. The deafening sound created a reverberating silence as he ran to Maria. He caught her before she dropped to the ground as Grant fell against the wall behind them.

The three officers rushed in to disarm and check on Grant and Patrick. Two surrounded Grant as he clung to the wound on his knee. Patrick hadn't moved since the officer's bullets had rung through the warehouse. Sam hurried in, followed by two paramedics. One dropped to his knees beside Grant while the other raced toward Maria.

Aeron held her tightly in his arms. Her skin was impossibly pale. Her eyes were fluttering as tears flowed freely. Her breathing was quick and labored. She was in rough shape.

Aeron wiped her auburn hair out of her hazel eyes; the dark flecks of dried blood were plastering it to her cheeks. There was a large bump on the side of her head. She shifted to look up into Aeron's eyes, flinching as she moved.

"Patrick?" she asked quietly.

Aeron wasn't sure what exactly she was asking. Looking over his shoulder, Aeron saw Sam tying a tourniquet around Patrick's leg. Making eye contact with the older man, Sam nodded. The bastard would be fine.

"Shhh, Maria. We need to get you to a hospital," he said, looking her over.

She had blood smeared across her cheeks and down her legs where the velour pants were torn, and he could see bruising all over her body. The paramedic was preparing her for a stretcher.

"The other girls!" she cried.

"Maria, I will explain everything soon. Please try to stay calm," Aeron said, squeezing her shoulder lightly to reassure her.

Maria, Patrick, and Grant were loaded into ambulances and taken to the closest hospital.

Chapter
Thirty-Eight
Maria, July 6th

Maria awoke to the steady tune of mechanical beeping. She turned her head to the side and blinked slowly, bringing the room into focus. Slumped in sleep, both her parents were crammed into a double chair. Her mother's head was resting on her father's chest while her father's head hung back, resting on the wall.

Maria wondered how long she had been out. Looking around, she noticed the machinery making the beeping sounds that had pulled her from her sleep. The black monitor showed her the proof of life with the green jumps on the screen. An IV stand sat next to the bed and hooked into her arm. Turning to the other side, she saw a small table full of flowers and cards.

Swallowing hard, she wished she had a drink. Her throat was dry, and each swallow felt like sandpaper. Taking a deep breath, she looked down the length of her body. She had more bandages on her than she ever remembered having. Her wrists were wrapped, as were her knees, and she could feel something plastered to the underside of her right eye.

Taking a deep breath, she grimaced. Grant must have broken a rib when he kicked her on the warehouse floor. Tentatively, she reached a hand to her head and found another bandage on her forehead. She wasn't sure which blow to the head had caused the need for that one. The last thing she remembered was Grant asking Aeron if he was a cop. Even now, she was shocked by Aeron's answer. It explained so much. Peering around her sterile room, she was saddened to see he wasn't there.

Groaning, she dropped her arm from her head. Her entire body ached. She felt like she had after running a 5k that had far too many obstacles several years ago—no, this was worse. She missed when her biggest issue in life was deciding what she was going to do each weekend.

Despite the pain, she longed to get up and stretch her legs. Forcing herself into a sitting position, she flinched at the pain shooting through her abdomen. With a sharp release of breath, she swung her legs to the floor. Looking down at her feet, she noticed the bright-yellow socks. Fancy.

Pushing herself to her feet, she held her breath as she stood. At the moment her bottom left the bed, a loud alarm sounded. She didn't have time to contemplate the reason before her parents were awake and two nurses raced into the room.

"Miss Hernandez," said a kindly older woman as she took Maria's forearm into one hand as the other nurse did the same on the other side. "You're a fall risk, sweetie. You can't get out of bed without someone else with you." The two women forced her back onto the bed.

"Oh, Maria dear. How are you feeling, darling?" her mother asked from over one of the nurse's shoulders.

She looked up at her mother, whose vibrant eyes were red and swollen. Sitting back on the bed, she met her father's eyes. They had dark circles below. He was examining her face, checking for who knew what. The signs of the physical trauma she'd endured were quite evident, but she knew there would be emotional trauma as well.

Maria turned back to the nurse by her side. "What?"

"You have three broken ribs, a concussion with a large gash to your forehead, some serious bruising, and cuts on your wrists. Those will probably scar. Lastly, you have a very slight fracture to your right kneecap. You will have difficulty straightening and putting weight on that leg," the nurse said and nodded down at the aforementioned leg.

Looking down and lifting the gown, she found a brace tightly wrapped around the knee. She'd thought it was just a wrap around her knee.

"I need you to stay in bed, sweetie," the older of the two nurses insisted as she patted Maria on the shoulder and left the room.

Maria nodded, unable to absorb all she had been told. The movement felt like she was about to jostle her brain out of its proper position. "The other girls," she whispered to no one in particular. "Are... Are they okay?" she asked, her voice cracking.

"Aeron asked to be called, and he will explain everything to you," her mother said, not quite meeting her eyes. "But yes, they're all right. The police are going to need to get your official statement as well." A tear slid down her mother's face.

Maria couldn't imagine what she'd felt when she was told what had happened.

"Patrick?" Maria asked, looking to her father. If the news was as grim as she expected, she didn't want her mother to be the one who had to break the news.

He sat straighter in his chair; she could see the pain etched throughout his features as his face contorted. "He survived, but he will never be a free man again."

She wasn't sure how she should feel. Should she be glad her brother survived, or should she have wished death upon him like he had her? The conflicting emotions had her feeling wretched. She wasn't sure if he would survive. There was so much blood on the floor. She'd been terrified when Grant forced her out onto the warehouse floor, keeping her body pressed to his. She'd tried to fight him, to get away from him and over to the officers. To Aeron.

She nodded, glancing between her parents, then choked out, "I'm so sorry."

"Oh, dear, it wasn't your fault," her mother said through her tears.

Although she had always cared about her brother, tears were not forthcoming. She felt guilty for never understanding why her brother hated her so much. If she had tried to understand him more, maybe this wouldn't have happened. She let her chin fall to her chest, already wishing she were still sleeping.

Before she was allowed the luxury of sleep, an officer entered the room and introduced himself as he settled in to get her official statement. Annoyed this couldn't wait until later, she gave her parents the signal that she was okay to answer his questions alone. Speaking for as long as she did was headache inducing. The officer gave her his contact info before leaving, instructing her to call him if she remembered anything more of significance. Tipping her head back to rest on the pillows, she closed her eyes again, willing the pain of her reality to melt away with her consciousness.

When she awoke, the room was dim. The only light came from the television, which cast an eerie hue around the room. Pushing herself up onto her elbows, she felt that twinge in her ribs. The chair her parents had shared earlier in the afternoon was now occupied by another. His face was pinched as if he were hurting purely from looking at her.

He stood from the chair and stalked over to her. Snaking one hand around the back of her head, he gently laced his fingers through her hair as he tipped his head down to press his forehead tentatively against hers. His other arm pressed into the mattress by her hip. He breathed her in.

"I was so damn worried about you, Maria. Patrick knocked me out while we were in the club. I had no idea how much time had passed. Sam came to find me when he saw Patrick taking you away." He shook his head. "I am so fucking sorry. None of this needed to happen."

She had so many questions but settled on just one. "Aeron?" she asked then waited for him to make eye contact with her. When he removed his forehead from hers to look her in the eyes, she felt the loss deep in her soul. "Are you a cop?"

"FBI," he said simply.

She released the breath she didn't realize she was holding. His answer meant more to her than she wanted to admit. He was in that place for necessity, not for the same sick reasons as Grant or Patrick. "How did you get involved in all that?"

"That is a long story, Maria. Are you sure you're up for it tonight?"

With a cringe, she sat up straighter in her bed. "I am."

Sighing, Aeron sat on the side of the bed, facing her. "You know I didn't have the best relationship with my parents or the greatest childhood in general, for that matter," he said without waiting for her to confirm. "But I did have a cousin, Sage. I didn't get to see her much after I got into high school and certainly not while I was at college. But when I moved away after college, it was to be closer to her. She reached out to me on social media because neither of us had the other's phone number. Anyway, she messaged, and she was asking odd questions. I quickly became concerned. She wanted to know if I knew how the court system worked for various crimes. She told me it was for a class, and she just wanted to ask me to see if she was understanding the material."

Maria couldn't stop herself from fidgeting as she listened.

"I didn't like the feeling I got, so I moved back to be closer to her." He scoffed, but she could hear the pain in his voice as he recounted the story.

Reaching out, she took his hand in hers. She felt a gentle squeeze as he continued.

"I didn't find out the real reason until months after I had been back. I stopped by to visit her one night. Wednesday nights were supposed to be our catchup nights, but she was drunk. And in that drunken state, she told me about when she was a freshman at a college in North Carolina. She went to a back-to-school party with a large group of people. One thing led to another, and she thought she was raped. She woke up in a strange house with her skirt pushed up around her waist. She was terrified. She'd been too afraid to call the police." Aeron's eyes misted as he took a moment to clear his throat.

"When I started prodding her, asking what she did afterward, she just looked at me blankly. As if I made the entire thing up and hadn't heard her correctly. I wanted her to be able to trust me, but it was as if the moment she realized what she said, she laughed it off. Tried to make it seem like it was nothing or that I misunderstood what she was trying to say. I don't think I've ever seen someone do that before, drunken confessions. This was serious. She didn't do anything about it. She just ran away. That pissed me off. If I hadn't shown up that night, she probably never would have told me." He scoffed, running his hands through his dark hair. "I don't think she remembered telling me. But after that, I watched how she interacted with other people. Tried to study and see if I could discern any telltale signs."

Maria could see how deeply this still bothered him. "Is she why you wanted to be an agent?"

He met her with a half-smile. "Partially. I always wanted to be a cop, especially with how nothing ever happened with my father." Nodding, he paused while he thought about his story.

Waiting patiently, Maria moved her hand to Aeron's thigh.

"When I started watching Sage, I could tell she was careful whenever she went out. She limited the number of drinks she had and always made sure she had someone to watch a drink if she used the bathroom. She was a good kid. I had to go back to college for only a year and a half to complete all the classes I needed, joined the police academy, and one thing led to another, and I became an agent.

"Sage was going on a solo road trip after she graduated. I think she wanted to prove to herself that she could. Throughout the remainder of her college career, she always operated in a buddy system. She wanted to experience the U.S. as much as she could before finding a career." He shook his head as if trying to deny the past. "She called me one night, telling me about this guy she met at the bar. This guy sounded too good to be true. She wanted to send me a picture of him. You could have blown me over when I received the picture. Leaning over a bar behind her was your brother. He looked like he was placing an order or something." Aeron dropped the bomb on her, and she lost the ability to breathe.

"She became one of his first victims." If Maria thought she couldn't breathe before, it was worse now. "She was missing for six months before she was able to force her way out of the house. The man had a wife." Aeron released a breath. "She stumbled upon some old woman's house early one morning, and the woman thought Sage was going to attack her. She was bruised from head to toe. She was wearing nothing but skimpy lingerie when the police got to her. She was frantic, constantly looking over her shoulder. Nothing came of what happened to her. She was unable to articulate what happened coherently. But I understood the gist of what happened."

Aeron's voice cracked, and he paused to compose himself. "It took me a while, but eventually, my boss let me get ahold of your brother and get myself a job with him. It started with me working at the motel, and then I quickly moved up in his ranks. With each new position, hiding my real job became more difficult. It came to the point where I needed another agent there to have my back, hence Sam."

"Is Sam also an officer?" The faint headache still radiating through her mind caused the pieces of Aeron's story to compile more slowly.

He nodded. "Sam joined me, and we began planting trackers in the tracksuits and the hair clips the girls are given at the nightclub. We were able to track them after they got bought. Then when the girls started going missing from the homes of the men who bought them, they started blaming your brother. The backlash pissed him off. These men all had money, and they were more than just a little angry. Your brother didn't know how it happened, but he was beginning to suspect it was because of me."

Maria could feel something churning in her gut as she thought of all the women her brother had abducted and others had tried to rescue. "What happened to Sage?" she asked, afraid of what she would hear.

Aeron paused, and she gave his hand an encouraging squeeze. "She couldn't escape the demons she was forced to live with after those horrendous months. I tried to get her to go to therapy to talk with someone about it, but she felt there was something wrong with her, that no one would want to be around a woman like her. She ended all the pain for herself." A tear slid down Aeron's cheek. "I never forgave your brother for what he did to her."

"I don't think I could have either," Maria admitted. "I can't forgive what I've seen. What I experienced at his hand."

"That's why when you asked me to keep you out of the trailer, I couldn't force you in with the others. It was bad enough watching what happened to each of them every day. I couldn't stand to watch something happen to someone I care about again."

Maria yawned as she nodded. "I'm sorry," she said, covering the yawn with her hand. "I just have one more question." She forced her eyes to stay open. "What happened to the other girls?"

"There was a bust set up to take place at each of the locations that day. All the women who had been in the trailer with you were taken from the nightclub. They are all recovering, and the men working for Patrick have been taken into custody—all of them. The men bidding on the girls have been arrested too."

She began to shake as tears racked her body, and she tried to suppress hiccups. "Jenny?"

"Shhh, her body has been brought to her family. Her lost life was nothing we could have predicted, and I promise you, I would have done anything to save her," he said, shifting on the bed to align his body with hers. Helping to brace her body, he helped her lie down as he took up the small space next to her. The last thing she remembered was thinking she was finally safe.

EPILOGUE
CASSIDY, THREE WEEKS LATER, JULY 26TH

Cassidy wondered if the tears would ever subside. She knew she was lucky to have survived, but losing one of her best friends would haunt her for the rest of her life. She had made a promise to stick with Jenny and keep her safe. She should have convinced Jenny to see reason. Then, perhaps they would be together today.

Another round of tears fell from her tender eyes.

Today was the first time she'd left her parents' house in more than two weeks. She was terrified of everything around her now. She felt people were walking too close to her. She didn't know if she would ever go to another bar in her life, never mind take a drink from someone else.

She had dropped out of college; she needed a break. Everyone around her knew what had happened. They constantly asked her if she was okay and told her they were sorry to hear about what had happened. She was worried classmates would stare at her, like they were waiting for her to have a total breakdown.

Looking down at the program spread out over her lap, she recognized the picture as one she had taken on the last trip Jenny had taken with her family. Seeing the smile on Jenny's face looking up at her, Cassidy let a small, sad smile escape. Cassidy had been allowed to attend, as usual. Being the only person who knew the truth, she usually tagged along. It was wonderful.

Another tear dropped. It fell onto Jenny's cheek, as if she were crying too.

Cassidy jumped as a hand rested gently on her wrist. It was Maria. She was beautiful, with her auburn hair pulled into a neat bun. There were scars around the edge of her face and along her wrists. Aeron sat next to her. Maria's face was filled with compassion—that didn't make her want to recoil. "Do you mind if I sit with you for a moment?"

Cassidy shook her head.

"I am so sorry for what my brother did to you all. If you ever need someone to talk to, please let me know. I will always be here." Maria's voice cracked as she spoke. She took a deep, calming breath as she kept one hand on Cassidy's wrist.

Aeron leaned forward. She had learned about his double life while she was in the hospital. He and another officer had stopped in to explain everything that would be happening in the coming months and years. She was going to be tied to this case until all the men involved were sentenced, unless they all took plea deals, which she doubted. She would likely be forced to sit on a witness stand and recount the most terrifying days of her life.

"I understand the loss you're feeling. And I'm sorry about your friend. I wish we had been able to stop them before you girls were taken." Aeron's head dropped. "Jenny's life was senselessly lost."

Cassidy furrowed her brow, trying to keep the new wave of tears at bay. "It was her heart, you know? They did an autopsy. She had a heart condition, and her heart gave out." Cassidy sniffled as she spoke.

Maria handed her a tissue, and she took it with a small smile.

"Thanks," she said, wiping away the tears. The knowledge that Jenny had died in her sleep was comforting.

"Are you getting out much?" Maria asked. "You should really consider the counseling."

Cassidy knew this was coming from a good place. Maria had done more than any of the rest of them when it came to trying to escape.

Cassidy bobbed her head in a noncommittal nod, somehow feeling a new wave of calm. She was distraught over Jenny's death, but she felt like she could now have a future again. She'd refused to attend the recommended counseling, but maybe Maria was right. Maybe she did need to go. Jenny wouldn't be happy to see her give up and become a recluse.

When a motion at her side caught her eye, she saw two more people standing at the edge of their row. Hannah and Kenzie stood there, looking vastly different from the last time she'd seen them all dolled up in a Vegas club.

Hannah and Kenzie were solemn. She wanted to blame Kenzie for Jenny's demise, but she knew it wouldn't be fair. They would forever be bonded over their distressing past—trauma.

"Thank you for talking with me." Cassidy paused to look them each in the eyes.

Maria nodded then leaned forward to give her a hug. "Everything will be okay. Please reach out if you ever want to talk," she whispered as she rubbed Cassidy's back.

Aeron shook her hand. Standing, they each greeted Kenzie and Hannah. Maria gave them each a hug and asked them to reach out if they ever needed to. They left to find seats at the back of the hall. Aeron walked with his hand at Maria's lower back.

Kenzie and Hannah sat on either side of Cassidy. Interlacing their arms with one another, they wept for the lost soul. They were all grateful for their safety. And yet they carried vast guilt. It niggled in the back of her mind each day. She felt worse because she was holding a secret from them all. There was one man missing from the arrest list, one who'd threatened her life if she ever revealed his identity. Shaking off the thought, she focused on the moments to come. She needed to give this time to Jenny's memory.

They all looked ahead as the funeral began.

Thank You for Reading!

If you have enjoyed this book, please follow E. Lynn on her various social media accounts for more author content or sign up for her newsletter on her website!

Facebook: Author E. Lynn
Instagram: @e.lynn.author
TikTok: E.Lynn
Website: www.authorelynn.com

ACKNOWLEDGMENTS

Thank you for choosing my novel to read. This was one I began writing during the end of the pandemic. I was working for a company that required that people's temperatures be taken when they arrived at work, and the job required me to man a desk for several hours with nothing to do but take people's temperatures. So I must say thank you to that part-time job that let my mind wander and create this story for you all. Not sure how my mind makes it to these strange situations, but here we are.

I then would like to thank my mother and sisters again for their critical eyes and willingness to help me in this journey. I can say that it was not easy getting used to people who know me reading my writing the first time, and I am lucky to say that this time was even easier. Even though my stories seem to range in their content, I hope they will be ready for all the stories to come and will continue to be in my corner.

I would also like to thank everyone from Red Adept Editing for their assistance. The editors and proofreaders helped me to create something that I hope will pull you readers in. Their criticisms have helped me to grow as a writer and have given me so much to think about when I work on my future stories. I hope to work with you all for a while to come. This book actually started as what I had planned to be a romantic suspense tale. However, after the feedback from my content editor, I decided to change almost the entire story.

Last but certainly not least, I would like to thank my husband for always being by my side. He has helped me to find where I can improve my stories by asking helpful questions about my plots. For this book in particular, he helped me do some research and think more about the background of a human trafficking scheme and how it might work. Whether he knows it or not, he will likely continue to be my sounding board. Ahh, the shackles of marriage...

I hope you will continue on this publishing journey with me.

About the Author

E. Lynn has loved reading since her mother read books to her as a child. Something about being able to get lost in a book took hold of her imagination. It was not until the pandemic, spending long days and weeks at home, did she begin writing. She found a release in letting out the ideas that clogged her mind. As one story swam to the surface others would find their way into the pool of possibilities. With many more novel ideas on the horizon, E. Lynn hopes to pull people in with her own stories of love, loss, and suspense.

She has lived in Vermont her entire life but has enjoyed traveling with her husband. They hope to do much more traveling when their children are older. So, until the day she can wake up and walk out to the beach each morning she will live vicariously through her characters.

Also by E. Lynn